Lizzy picked up a horseshoe and hooked a perfect throw that smacked against the peg.

"There!" she said, gloating. "Now if you'd put yours somewhere close to the peg, I'd be grateful. At least it would be a game instead of a giveaway on my part."

Trouble's horseshoe landed six inches from the peg. It was humiliating to look up. Lizzy's face returned contempt. So did her lips.

"Missed. What a surprise!" she sneered. "Old Red Face! I'll bet your mama thinks your red hair and brown eyes are beautiful, but they're not. You're ugly! Of all the boys around, you're the most repulsive. You ride around on your horse like you're a prince. People are supposed to bow down because *you're* a *Warden*. Well, guess what? When *I* see you, I eliminate you from my mind. You fade away in a flash."

Trouble's sister, Carrie, had told him once that when he lost his temper, his face got redder than his hair. At this minute he felt it must be glowing. The thought made him furious.

"All right, Lizzy, you asked for it. I used to like everybody in the settlement until you made me your special case to torment. But I don't care anymore. You say you can't stand to be around me? Well, you're not so great yourself. I don't like you, Lizzy Faraday, and I never will. You're the most unlikable girl I've ever known, and I've got a suggestion for you. It'll take a lot of work, but why don't you learn to be a lady?"

Lizzy's expression told Trouble he had hit his mark. He walked away—ecstatic.

FREDA CHRISMAN—In the Houston metroplex, their church, two children, and six grandchildren occupy the Chrismans' retirement. Prior to publishing her first novel with Heartsong Presents, Freda's articles and short stories appeared in Sunday school take-home papers and denominational magazines. A novella and four books later, she still praises the Lord that words edifying Him flow to her computer.

Books by Freda Chrisman

HEARTSONG PRESENTS
HP233—Faith Came Late
HP404—At the Golden Gate
HP539—Two Hearts Wait

Hearts
Twice Met

Freda Chrisman

Heartsong Presents

To Dr. and Mrs. Ron Lyles, the church staff, and members of South Main Baptist Church. Thank you!

A note from the Author:
I love to hear from my readers! You may correspond with me by writing:

Freda Chrisman
Author Relations
PO Box 719
Uhrichsville, OH 44683

ISBN 1-59310-743-9

HEARTS TWICE MET

Our mission is to publish and distribute inspirational products offering exceptional value and biblical encouragement to the masses.

PRINTED IN THE U.S.A.

prologue

Maryland, 1852

"You think because your old man's rich, you're better than the rest of us," screeched Lizzy Faraday. "You think you're smarter than me, too. Well, you're wrong! I may be poor, but I'm not dumb. In fact, I'm just as good as you are and just as smart!"

Trouble Warden, twelve, backed away from her accusing index finger. "I didn't say I was better than you. I've hardly said a word. You've done all the talking." Trouble couldn't keep from adding, "As usual."

Scorn swept Lizzy's face. "You did your share. All I said was you couldn't throw a horseshoe straight if they paid you." Trouble hated Lizzy's superior smile. Her long, blond braid slithered across her shoulders. Hands gripping her skinny hips, she pierced him with a stare. "You play tricks, too. Awhile ago you asked what books I liked. You know I don't have any books. You wanted to embarrass me and brag about yours."

Trouble had tried all day to keep away from Lizzy, whose delight was to initiate a good fight. If the fight was with him, so much the better. He was her favorite adversary.

He hadn't wanted to come to the annual picnic for the mill hands. He knew eleven-year-old Lizzy would be there. Her family was first in line every year. That's because there was plenty of food. The two Faraday brothers and Lizzy always seemed to be hungry.

The negative thought stung his conscience. Maybe they truly were hungry. He hadn't given the girl a fair chance, either. He'd better control his prejudice and face up to the facts.

First, he had to be there. Second, his father owned the mills, so naturally they provided the food. Third, he was one of the three Warden sons and had no choice but to attend.

Sufficiently chastened, he tried again. "Listen, I don't want to be here any more than you do. But here we are, and everybody's playing games and swimming, fishing, or talking. Let's just throw horseshoes and leave off the conversation. Is that possible?"

Lizzy's blue eyes took in the plainly dressed workers engaged in those pastimes around the open field. Trouble looked away, irritated with himself that he'd noticed the color of her eyes.

The grassy lot curved like a green carpet along the bank of a nearby stream, flowing in ripples toward Chesapeake Bay. The spring day had enticed three of the mill families with small children to rest after the activities of the morning. Following the free picnic lunch, where food overloaded tables constructed with planks laid across sawhorses, wives of the workers gathered to talk. Beneath a leafy hedgerow, the women spread blankets on the grass for the children's naps; and some, tired from the week's hard work, slept a few minutes, too.

Lizzy picked up a horseshoe and hooked a perfect throw that smacked against the peg.

"There!" she said, gloating. "Now if you'd put yours somewhere close to the peg, I'd be grateful. At least it would be a game instead of a giveaway on my part."

Trouble's horseshoe landed six inches from the peg. It was humiliating to look up. Lizzy's face returned contempt. So did her lips.

"Missed. What a surprise!" she sneered. "Old Red Face! I'll bet your mama thinks your red hair and brown eyes are beautiful, but they're not. You're ugly! Of all the boys around, you're the most repulsive. You ride around on your horse like you're a prince. People are supposed to bow down because *you're* a *Warden*. Well, guess what? When *I* see you, I eliminate you from my mind. You fade away in a flash."

Trouble's sister, Carrie, had told him once that when he lost his temper, his face got redder than his hair. At this minute he felt it must be glowing. The thought made him furious.

"All right, Lizzy, you asked for it. I used to like everybody in the settlement until you made me your special case to torment. But I don't care anymore. You say you can't stand to be around me? Well, you're not so great yourself. I don't like you, Lizzy Faraday, and I never will. You're the most unlikable girl I've ever known, and I've got a suggestion for you. It'll take a lot of work, but why don't you learn to be a lady?"

Lizzy's expression told Trouble he had hit his mark. He walked away—ecstatic.

one

Maryland, 1858

"Why, Elizabeth Faraday! How pretty you've grown! How old are you now? Seventeen, eighteen?"

Mary Nugent stopped the girl as she closed the door to the general store behind herself. Carrying a mesh shopping bag of groceries, the lady used her free hand to shade her eyes from the bright morning sun.

"I'm seventeen, ma'am," said Elizabeth, recognizing the mother of her friend, Graham.

"Can that be? Seems like only yesterday that Graham said you were fishing down at the old millpond."

Elizabeth tossed her thick braid of hair back over her shoulder. Her blue shirt was an outgrown hand-me-down from Fred, her younger brother. The color matched her eyes.

"I was a terrible tomboy in those days," Elizabeth admitted. "Being the only woman in our house, I guess I just naturally adopted that lifestyle. I hope I'm more of a lady now."

Mary laughed and linked arms with Elizabeth to walk along the short row of stores. "I should say you are. A lady with golden hair, brilliant blue eyes, and a lovely, heart-shaped face. I imagine every girl in the settlement is jealous of you."

Elizabeth felt her face burn. "Mrs. Nugent, you're embarrassing me. Nobody would be jealous of Elizabeth Faraday."

As if agreeing with her, a horse hitched to a nearby rail snorted and bobbed his head. The two laughed.

"Now don't sell yourself short, Miss Lizzy," said Mary. "I'll just have to convince you that I'm right."

Falling in step, they walked a few yards to the cobbler's shop. Mary went inside to pick up her husband's shoes that had been repaired, and Elizabeth followed. While the shoemaker gave the shoes a last brush, Mary spoke again.

"During the week, when he builds furniture, Riley wears a pair of clumpy old shoes that are comfortable," she explained. "These are his Sunday shoes. When he wears them with his good black suit and a starched white shirt, he's very handsome."

On the street again, two plainly dressed ladies stopped Mary Nugent to admire her dark gray morning dress. Balancing the shopping bag and the shoes on one arm, Mary turned to show them a hidden pocket in the skirt. Elizabeth smiled and took her things so Mary could finish her demonstration. Minutes later the ladies moved on, and Elizabeth spoke to distract Mary from taking her burden back.

"You must love your husband very much, Mrs. Nugent. Your face lights right up when you talk about him."

"Of course I love him. That's the way women feel about their husbands," she said, stepping aside to avoid a child running by with a sticky lollipop.

"No, not all women. My pa was mean to my mother when she was alive. I don't think he ever said a kind word to her."

"I'm sorry that's the way it was, dear. What a terrible memory." Stirring leaves on an overhead tree branch failed to mask Mary's frown, and Elizabeth wished she'd kept quiet.

"I guess I shouldn't have told. It just slipped out."

Mary placed her hand on the girl's arm. "Elizabeth, don't feel that way. You can tell me anything you like, and I'll never breathe a word. I was your mother's friend. Sometimes we just need to talk to other people to get rid of bad things in our minds. You come to me anytime you want."

Elizabeth searched Mary's face. The lady meant what

she was saying. Did that mean she could talk to Mary Nugent about some of the things only another woman would understand? She'd never had anyone to tell secrets to. With her pa and two brothers to cook and keep house for, she had little time to make friends with other girls her age. Yet it was a deeply felt wish.

On Sundays she'd seen young men escorting elegant young ladies in their best dresses, holding dainty parasols to keep off the sun. But those girls had no time to befriend a tomboy.

Once while she washed her brothers' clothes in the yard, she had a daydream of changing, overnight, into a graceful, charming girl with a ruffled parasol. The dream lasted several minutes. Then she finished the clothes, took a look at her roughened red hands, and reality came rushing back.

She spoke again to Mrs. Nugent to forget the path her mind had taken. "It's been wonderful to walk and talk with you this way, ma'am. Now I'd better get down to the Hellers' for a slab of bacon Pa spoke for last week. I said I'd pick it up before noon."

"All right, dear," Mary replied. "But I was just wondering. If we came by for you, would you go to church with us on Sunday? We'd love to have you, and we'll have lunch together."

"No. I don't have a Sunday dress, Mrs. Nugent. I couldn't go to church where all of you have clothes better than I've ever owned. Take the one you're wearing, for instance. Those ladies we met complimented you on it, and they called it a work dress. I have nothing better than what I'm wearing. Besides, I don't have time to worry about looking pretty. I have too much work to do. People have to take me as I am."

"Most people would consider themselves blessed to be acquainted with you. I certainly feel that way." Mary took the shoes Elizabeth held and tugged the shopping bag onto her other wrist. "Let me ask you a question. Would you come to church with us if you had a dress? If you'll let me, I can provide one. The last time she and Graham visited from Philadelphia, my daughter-in-law, Carrie, left one behind when they rushed off."

Her breathing shallow, Elizabeth gasped for air. Wonderful as it sounded, she couldn't accept. Her pa would scream that it was charity from one of those *aristocrats* again. And attend church with the Nugents? She didn't dare think about it.

"I. . .I don't think Pa would allow that, ma'am."

Mary leaned closer, whispering. "I know your father's problem, dear, and I know you don't have many pleasures to look forward to at home. Life in the Lord gives a believer constant pleasure, Elizabeth. We all have a choice to make, for Him or against Him, regardless of the circumstances. Won't you think about it and consider letting us take you to church? It doesn't matter what you wear. If your clothes are clean and neat, that's all that's necessary."

"Thank you. I'll try." With the sole of her shoe, Elizabeth scuffed an aimless pattern in the dirt path. "Is it the church the Mortimer Wardens attend?"

"Yes! Carrie's whole family goes there, too. Mortimer is one of our church leaders. He's such a kind man. His wife, Gwendolyn, is my very good friend."

Elizabeth gave a little smirk. "Too bad their son Travis doesn't take after his pa." She was surprised by Mary's chuckle.

"Are you two still feuding?"

"Oh, no! He's too good for our little community. He's been going to school in Baltimore the last two years. He comes back just often enough to keep track of his father's business so someday he can be rich as Croesus, too."

Mary laughed again. "Elizabeth, wherever did you hear the story of that old king? You surprise me."

"I'm not dumb, Mrs. Nugent. People think I am because Pa and my brothers talk loud and don't have any manners. But Mother taught me to read, and I borrow books from Miss

Stimpson and one or two other ladies. I don't understand all I read, but I read anyway. Someday I'll understand."

"I'm sure you will." Affectionately, Mary tucked an unruly strand of the girl's hair back over her ear. "I'm so glad we've had time to talk, Elizabeth. You go after your bacon now, but I hope you'll feel free to visit me soon. I'd like to be much better acquainted with you. We can have a cup of tea together, and I also have some books you might like to borrow."

Elizabeth could hardly believe what she was hearing. Just to visit in the Nugent home would teach her so much. She had heard of its use of pastel colors, and she longed to see how they were displayed. The furniture Mr. Nugent had crafted for their home was legendary, and the thought of seeing it for herself lifted her spirits. She felt lighter than a butterfly.

"I'd be honored to come, ma'am."

"Then let's set a date. Why don't you try to come for lunch next Monday?"

"I'll try, ma'am. I'll surely try."

After a warm good-bye, Elizabeth walked the tree-shaded path toward the Heller place to get the meat her father had spoken for. She hoped there would be no question about payment. Pa said he had done a favor for Jedidiah Heller, and Mr. Heller owed him the bacon slab. But he'd said that before. Sometimes when a supposed debt was to be paid, it was Elizabeth who took the brunt of a rejection by the other party plus the verbal abuse that went with it.

Today was her lucky day, and Mrs. Heller cheerfully hauled out the pork slab wrapped in oilskin. It was heavy, but Elizabeth managed to get it home and hung in the smokehouse before she continued the day's chores.

❧

At twilight, Sid Faraday stumbled through the door of their ramshackle house and threw his work hat on the floor. "Didja get that bacon from Jedidiah's today? Bet you forgot it. Just like you. Readin' all the time, never doin' what you're told."

Elizabeth didn't answer right away. Pa had been drinking. When he wasn't himself, he always criticized her unduly. She pulled out a chair from the kitchen table.

"Here, Pa. Sit yourself and rest. I can tell you've had a hard day. Don't worry about the bacon. It's hanging in the smokehouse."

Her brother, Fred, slipped in the door. "See there, Pa, I told you she'd go after it. Elizabeth takes good care of us."

"Oh, goody! You always put in a good word for her, don't ya? If you'd do your job as well as you hold up for her, you might get on at the mills regular. We could use some more comin' in." Gray-haired Sid's dark eyes held no compassion for either of them.

Sid swept a stern glance at his daughter as she turned the fish she was frying for supper. Potatoes and carrots cooked at the back of the iron cookstove. Elizabeth kept working, hoping Fred would keep down any conversation involving her.

"Where's your brother?" her father asked Fred.

"He went by the Spencers' to see if they had field work to do. I heard they put out the word at the mills."

"They won't take no thirteen-year-old boy. Not a skinny runt like him. What about you? Does the great Mortimer Warden think he can grant you work for the rest of the summer?"

"Caleb and Joshua both asked if I was available."

"Well, you can't take his sons' word for it. If the old man wants to hire somebody else, he will. Not one of those Wardens amounts to a pan of bread. I saw that youngest kid today, eatin' with the men, smilin' like he was their best friend. But he's not. Why, he'd as soon cut their throats as look at 'em."

Elizabeth watched Fred lower his head as if ashamed. "Travis is not bad, Pa. He's friendly," Fred murmured.

Stunned, Elizabeth held her temper. She wondered how he could forget. *It's just Fred's way. He doesn't remember the mean things Travis did when we were kids. When no one was looking, he called me "the ugly Faraday," and he'd ride his pony past me real close to scare me. And when he did something to make me angry, he always laughed! Pa's right about him. He's not worth a pan of bread!*

She took up the last of the golden brown fish and the seasoned vegetables she had cooked and carried them to the table. The hungry men began to eat the minute they took seats.

A moment later, a step thumped on the porch outside. Her younger brother, Charlie, bounded in. "How come you didn't wait for me?" he complained.

"I waited," said Elizabeth as she opened a jar of canned apples for their dessert.

"Is that supposed to make me feel better?" said Charlie, his tousled blond hair falling over aggressive green eyes. He laughed as if he'd made a good joke.

His father encouraged him with a laugh. Elizabeth wished she could get away from the laughter. It always followed when she tried to take part in their conversations.

She was dreaming again. She couldn't leave. Her family needed her too much. Besides, where would she go? She had no one but them.

Looking around the tiny house, she saw all its faults: the uninspired rough-cut furniture thrown together, curtains her mother had hung so long ago, a cabinet standing beside the stove, and wide-plank flooring whose grain had been scrubbed away. The rest was more of the same. Nothing in the place even resembled her young-girl dreams of a nice home.

Nor did she expect comfort from the three males at the table. Their personalities were different. Charlie simply followed her father's undisciplined example. Her father liked to verbally abuse Fred and her to make himself feel in control. Husky, fifteen-year-old Fred tried, but he hadn't the courage to stand up to the strong wills of the other two.

Elizabeth decided she needed something of her own. Mary Nugent's invitation to visit her was a chance to leave the house for a few hours. She'd go. She'd arrange her day on Monday so she'd be sure to have supper ready when the men got home. She'd extend herself and learn how Mary planned a lady's routine. For a thank-you, she'd take her hostess a plate of vanilla and walnut cookies. They were her best gift. Her heart raced as she reflected on the potential of the Monday visit.

❧

It was with a sense of pride that she finished her chores and set off for Mary Nugent's home on Monday morning. Though their home was meager in appeal, Elizabeth scrupulously kept the house clean.

Dishes were done, beds were made, beans were put to soak for supper. When she came home from her visit, she'd cook the beans with strips of bacon and bake a pan of corn bread to go with them. Elizabeth smiled in anticipation of her family's pleasure. It was one of their favorite suppers.

In a clean waist and a threadbare black skirt, she held herself as straight and tall as her five feet three inches would let her. She had nearly a mile to walk, so protecting Mary's tin of cookies, she picked a careful path on her way through the village.

A rain during the night had freshened leaves on the trees, and in the fields she passed, all her favorite wildflowers were bursting with color. The smell of the river in the distance recalled memories of her carefree childhood when her mother was alive.

Life had order and pleasure then. It wasn't so full of bitter days. They had been poor, but Mama made them feel rich.

She and Fred remembered. Charlie didn't, and Elizabeth's heart knew regret at the thought.

She passed along the main street, past the few shops that supplied the villagers with the necessities of their daily lives. A few people spoke to her, but she knew they did so because they knew she was a Faraday and felt sorry for her. Their sympathy had brought out a mean streak in her as a child, and she had fought back the way her father taught her. No wonder the town thought of her only as a tomboy.

Elizabeth straightened her shoulders and called up the poise just beginning to blossom within her. Ahead, a wide pool of water from the overnight rainfall cut her off from the path opposite. She started to walk around, found the way to her right impossible, and turned to the left.

Suddenly a spray of dirty water trickled down the black skirt she had worked so hard to render clean. She scowled at the driver of the fancy carriage and at the girl in a ruffled gingham bonnet at his side.

"Whoa! Whoa!" The horse halted, and the man jumped from the carriage. "Oh, ma'am! I *am* sorry!"

It was Travis Warden!

Elizabeth, close to tears, turned on him. "I should have known it was you. You did that on purpose!" Anger shook her attempt at calm. "Go away!"

Travis left his friend sitting alone and trotted around the puddle to stand tall before Elizabeth. "Are you all right, miss? You're not hurt, are you?" Realization of whom he had treated so badly suddenly dawned. His face paled from shock. "Lizzy! Lizzy Faraday! It's you!"

"Elizabeth to you, sir." She drew herself up stiffly to impress him with her cool manner. "You've ruined my appearance, but I'm not hurt, thank you," she said frostily. "I'll be on my way now." She stepped around the muddy pool the way he had come and strode quickly along toward Mary Nugent's house.

"Wait! We'll take you wherever you're going. I feel responsible." The hat Travis had taken off in her presence went back on his head, and he followed her a few feet.

"Travis!" called the pretty girl in the carriage. "Where are you going? Don't just leave me sitting here."

Six-foot-tall Travis Warden stood between the two girls, looking back and forth like a child caught in a position of complete despair.

Five minutes before, Elizabeth's angry heart had no smile to give. Now she left the scene with her shoulders shaking in soundless laughter.

two

Elizabeth hurried through the gate to the Nugent front door. Through the years, she'd admired their home from a distance but had never been up close. Flowers bloomed in neat beds around the house, and she imagined Mary finding pleasure in setting them out each spring. She was so carried away by the thought that she almost forgot the embarrassing state of appearance Travis Warden had forced her to.

Mary opened the door at her knock. "Come in, Elizabeth, come in. I'm glad you found time for a visit."

Her hostess's blue dress matched the pastel colors of her home. No wonder her excellent taste was the subject of so much talk in town. Bright flowers and scenic views were popular choices for wallpaper in other homes. Some women thought them the height of good taste. Nevertheless, it was the Nugent home that was looked upon as the essence of warmth and welcome.

Elizabeth wondered how soon Mary would notice her soiled skirt. It was best to mention it herself.

"I had an unfortunate accident on the way here. Travis Warden took time for me out of his busy schedule of squiring girls about town. He ran through a mud puddle and splashed water on my skirt. I'm sorry I look so untidy."

Mary leaned over to examine the skirt. "That's terrible, Beth! Did he apologize?"

Beth? Beth! How charming! I will never again think of myself as Elizabeth. Even if no one but Mary Nugent ever calls me that, I'll always be Beth inside.

With embellishments, *Beth* told Mary the story of Travis's

dilemma as she left him in the middle of the street, and Mary laughed until she could laugh no more. She warmed a flatiron, and with a good brushing and pressing while wearing one of Mary's robes, Beth brought the skirt back to its worn-out state of cleanliness.

Later, after a light lunch in the Nugents' sitting room, the tin of cookies Beth had brought complemented their tea.

"These are tasty, Beth. Very good. Do you mind if I call you Beth? I talk too fast to handle your longer name continually. Furthermore," the lady added, "I think you look like a Beth—down-to-earth, amiable, and straightforward."

Beth giggled. "Then to you I'll be Beth forever. Elizabeth will answer only to strangers."

After the dishes were done, Mary invited her to her bedroom to see a quilt she was making. The spread incorporated the pastel colors her hostess had used to decorate the room.

"Oh, ma'am, it's so beautiful! Imagine creating something like this. I wish I could do one even half so pretty."

"If you'd like to learn, I'll try to teach you."

"I would. Very much."

In her heart Beth vowed that she *would* learn. One day she would create a quilt herself.

The two women sat in the window seat at a corner window. Beyond, the view was of a long green lawn bordered by flowering shrubs, and in the distance sparkled a pond surrounded by weeping willows and ornamental rocks.

"I have another reason for inviting you to this room, Beth. It shames you that you have no dress to wear. I can remedy that if you'll let me. Graham's sweet wife, Carrie, left dresses here that she doesn't plan to wear anymore. Believe me, this is true. I mentioned it in a foolish way earlier because I didn't want to hurt your feelings. If you don't take them, the clothes will be taken to the church and given away. Why shouldn't you have them?"

Beth was at the point of tears. Why shouldn't she have them? It hurt to refuse. "Ma'am, Pa would never let me wear them. He says everyone thinks they're better than our family. He says taking charity from rich people is worse than begging."

Mary jumped to her feet. Pressing her palm to her forehead, she paced the floor and exclaimed, "What an idea! Beth, we're all God's children in His eyes, and He's the One who matters. He wants us to take care of each other and to share, when we have the ability, with anyone who has a need."

"I'm sorry, Mrs. Nugent. Pa's set in his ways about not accepting charity from people. He wants respect, he says, and taking charity makes you poor."

"Nonsense! He should let his daughter be the flower of the family. He would get more respect that way than drinking with a crowd of men who just want him to buy their alcohol."

Beth's mouth dropped open in surprise. "No, ma'am, you're wrong. We don't have money to buy spirits for his friends. We need every bit of his salary just to get by."

Seating herself again, Mary took Beth's hand. "I'm telling you the truth, Beth. I'm sorry, but perhaps it's best you learn it from me than from others. You may be the only one who doesn't know the extent of your father's drinking. I wouldn't lie to you about such a thing." She brushed Beth's cheek. "But let's forget that for now. I'd like to see you at least try on one of the dresses I have. Won't you?"

More than anything, Beth wanted, just once, to look like a lady—as Mary did even in a work dress. "Well, I. . ."

Quickly, Mary opened the closet door and took out a rosy maroon dress that hung prominently in front. She handed it to Beth. "I'm going to run downstairs for a moment while you change into the dress, and I'll help you with the sash when I get back. Take your time."

The cloth felt like satin to Beth, who had never touched

so fine a material. Did she dare put it on? She had to, or her friend would be hurt. She didn't have to accept the dress. A few seconds, and that would be all. She just wanted to see how it felt to wear such a luxurious garment.

Her own clothes fell in a pile, and she stepped out of them. Of course she had no appropriate undergarment to wear with fine clothing, so she couldn't do it full justice. As she slipped into the maroon frock with its white, crocheted trim around the yoke, she thought how lucky Mary Nugent's daughter-in-law was to own such a dress.

Yet, because she was Mortimer Warden's daughter and Graham Nugent's wife, she must own many dresses just as pretty. What would it be like to be so spoiled? Carrie Nugent must be spoiled—look at her brother, Travis Warden. How spoiled he was.

The dress fell in place, and Beth chanced a glimpse at a long, framed looking glass at the end of the room. It gave back a clear reflection. She wasn't used to such finery. The dress fit her as if it were her own, and the image the mirror reflected took her breath away.

At a knock on the door, her benefactress slipped inside and palmed her cheeks at what she saw. "Beth! How beautiful you look! I knew you would. We must make plans for you to wear it to church."

Beth stepped back and started to unbutton the dress. "No, I can't do that. I tried it on because I wanted to see how it felt to wear a lovely dress for once. Now that I've done it, I'm satisfied. I don't need to go to church to feel pretty."

"That's not the reason Christians go to church, Beth. I go because believers in Christ Jesus need to assemble themselves together for encouragement in order to carry on God's work. The Bible tells us that. *I* want you to come with us to experience the love and peace a body of His people can extend to you."

Beth's heart was touched, and she really wanted to go with the Nugents, but it was not possible. *I need to get away before she talks me into something Pa would hold against me for the rest of my life.*

She sat in a chair, reached for her skirt, and pulled it on under the loosened dress. Mary helped her take off the maroon creation and turned her back as Beth put on her old waist. But Mary could not disguise her despair when she hung the beautiful dress in the closet again.

"Beth, it is not fair for you to be denied every person's right to worship." She put her arms around the girl and bowed her head. "Dear God, please help us work out this problem. Make a way for Beth to come to church with Riley and me so she can find faith in You that will give her abundant life only You can give. Thank You, Father. In Jesus' blessed name. Amen."

When Beth left to go home, new awareness had found a place in her heart. She didn't understand all her friend had said, but she knew now that until she did understand it, she'd never be content.

❧

Sally Wickstan had changed some since he went away, but Travis Warden still felt she was one of the silliest girls in the settlement. She'd laughed for an hour about Lizzy Faraday leaving him red-faced and trying to avoid a mud puddle. He failed to see any humor in it.

He drove the horse and buggy into the barn lot to be taken care of by a handler and made his way up the path to the stone house that was the Warden home. Meeting Lizzy, or Elizabeth, as she had politely informed him she preferred, had been a big surprise. As a matter of fact, she seemed to be blossoming into a bona fide human being.

With his time at home divided between his family, the Warden mills, and the church, he was busy. Each trip back had meant getting into a different routine. The rules of Baltimore contrasted markedly with life in his parents' home. Here, he lived by the family's schedule.

As if to prove his point, Mortimer Warden swung open the back door of the house. "You're back! Good. I've been waiting for you. We need to get down to the gristmill to check this afternoon's run. I want you to manage it on your own. The contract is with Samuel Black."

Rushing toward the front, his father's girth held him back but little. His hat was already in his hand to leave.

"I'll be there directly, Father. I should speak to Mother before I take off again. Sally's luncheon with her folks took longer than I'd thought, and I'd promised Mother to spend some time with her today. I'll go make my excuses."

"All right. I'll wait in the buggy. I want to catch the handler before he unharnesses." Always quick, Mortimer was out the door and gone before Travis reached the landing of the kitchen stairs.

He knocked at the door of his mother's sitting room and heard her welcoming voice. "I have to delay our time together, Mother," Travis apologized as he entered the snug little room. "Father wants me at the gristmill to watch a run this afternoon, and I just got home from the Wickstans' luncheon. I'm sorry." Placing a brief kiss on her forehead, he squeezed her hand.

"I'm disappointed, but your father wants you to learn the business. I'm sure he thinks it's necessary for you to be on hand, or he wouldn't have asked. Did you enjoy being with the Wickstans?"

"Umm, it was a very nice lunch."

"But you don't care for Sally."

"She *is* pretty silly, Mother."

"I think you're right. Carrie's friends seemed so much more sensible than girls are now. I doubt your father has ever been directly exposed to Sally's silliness, or he wouldn't have encouraged you to go. Her parents are members of our church."

"Yes, I know, but there are surely other girls in town who are more like Carrie," he said in anguish.

"Travis, you will probably never meet a girl you admire as much as your sister. You and she have a special relationship. She's a good wife to Graham, too."

"He deserves her. He's building quite a reputation in his law practice, you know. He's well known around Philadelphia. He and Carrie are both true servants of the Lord, Mother, but I'm sure you know that. They think I should move up there and attend the University of Pennsylvania. Carrie even asked me to live with them so I would be with family. It doesn't sound too bad, does it?"

Having laid aside her sewing when Travis came in, Gwendolyn rose, put her arms around his waist, and leaned against her tall son's chest. "Travis, you'll be farther away than you were in Baltimore. In my heart, I've held the dream that since you are so close to the Lord, you would end up as pastor of a church close to home. Your father and I would like that very much."

With a slender hand, Travis pressed her to his chest and lowered his chin to her graying hair. "Mother, you have Caleb and Joshua and Virgie close. Father believes I'll go into the mills—another choice. I may end up doing that, but you know I'm praying for the Lord's will in my profession. I expect Him to lead me directly to what He wants. In the long run, isn't that what you and Father both want?"

"Yes, of course," said Gwendolyn. "But it's hard to think of the difficult path you may trod."

&

Though their time together was limited, over the next few weeks, Beth and Mary Nugent became close friends. So motivated was she by the high level of well-being Mary gave her, Beth found various excuses to get away to benefit and learn from both the Nugents. Mary's husband was as endearing as his wife.

Beth tried, but she could not bring herself to try a Sunday morning trip to their church. Then June brought an extraordinary day when Sid announced a plan to take the boys on a Sunday fishing trip. He bragged that his friend owned a boat and that they would fish the entire day on Chesapeake Bay. Once she got past her concern that the friend's boat might not be at all seaworthy, Beth began to think of the possibilities.

"You can git caught up on your work while we're gone. With all this runnin' back and forth to town you've been doin' lately, you're gettin' behind. Don't think I've not noticed how lazy you've been."

Fred spoke quickly from his seat on the porch steps. "She's not lazy, Pa. Lizzy does as good as any woman. She ought to get out more. Who'll she find to marry if she don't?"

Sid Faraday howled with laughter from his old chair on the porch, his jug of spirits at hand. "Who'd have 'er? Ain't nobody goin' to marry Lizzy. She's too plain. Ain't too smart, neither."

Her father blinked a backward glance at her to see, Beth was sure, if he'd hurt her feelings. She lowered her lashes and kept her gaze on the sewing in her lap.

"Besides, she can't marry," he added drolly. "She has to stay at home and keep house for us while we work."

Fred walked a few feet away, gripping his hands as he spoke. "She has a right to marry, Pa. You can't expect the girl to stay here the rest of her life. Charlie and me will marry someday, and she should, too."

Charlie was half-asleep in the tall grass growing beside the porch. "Me marry? Not me. I'm never gettin' married."

Sid wandered down the porch steps muttering, "Nobody gets married without my say-so. Remember that!"

Charlie stared at the other two for a second; then he jumped up and followed his pa down the path away from the house, toward town. He never looked back.

"Don't believe him, Lizzy. You're gettin' to be a real pretty girl. Lots of folks think so," Fred murmured as soon as they were alone.

"You're trying to make me feel better, Fred. Pa's right. Probably no one will want me." Beth folded the shirt she'd patched and leaned forward on her stool, ready with a question. "Who are these 'lots of folks' who think I'm pretty?"

Chuckling, Fred took his pa's chair. "The O'Neil twins and Ned Tracy. The other day, at the mill, I heard them talkin' while they ate." He chuckled again. "Ned said he'd come courtin' if only he could be sure you wouldn't throw a rock at him."

Beth snorted. "Ned Tracy! I'll lay in a supply of rocks!"

Fred laughed, and Beth joined in. It was a good feeling. She couldn't remember the last time they had laughed together. Only with the Nugents did she ever feel free to laugh. Even so, an idea flashed through her mind.

"Can you keep a secret, Fred?"

"I reckon."

"Do you know the Nugents? They live over by the Byers's house."

"The furniture maker? Sure, I know of them, but I've never spoken to them." He slid her a guarded glance. "Have you?"

Beth got up and stood close. "Mary Nugent has become my friend," she whispered. "They want to pick me up to go to church with them."

"Lizzy! Will you go?" he asked in a whisper.

"Oh, I really want to, Fred. Did I tell you they call me Beth? I love being called Beth. I wish everyone called me that."

"Then I'll call you Beth when Pa and Charlie aren't around."

Beth's eyes misted when Fred gave her a little hug. Was

he as starved for affection as she'd found she was? Her arms went around him only for an instant. It would never do for Pa or Charlie to see that, either.

Fred stepped back and fiddled with a vine crawling up the side of the porch. "Do you think you'll go to church with them?"

"I was thinking I could get by with it the day you're all fishing on the bay. Mrs. Nugent even has a dress for me to wear."

"That'd be good. You want to know *my* secret?" Beth nodded, and he continued. "I've wanted to go to that church all my life."

"Oh, Fred," she said. "Maybe there's a way. There has to be a way."

three

Although she had bathed before she left the house, at the Nugents' Beth freshened up in a lovely bathing room with white walls and a border of pale pink roses and soft green leaves. In the room assigned her, she slipped into a borrowed petticoat and the maroon dress she had eagerly waited to wear to the Nugents' church.

She found another mirror in the room she was using, and she examined herself from head to toe. Her shoes, too, were a gift from Mary. She found the cobbler had estimated her size from the one and only time she had been in his shop. The mirror reflected the shine of her blond hair and the sparkle of her excited blue eyes. She wished Fred could see her. She felt pretty. A knock sounded at the door, and Beth answered.

"You look beautiful, Beth, and here's something to make you even prettier. My mother gave it to me when I married, and I want you to have it." She held out a brooch made of ivory that was the perfect throat ornament for the trim line of her bodice.

The lump in Beth's throat nearly choked her, yet she shook her head. "I want to wear it today, but I can't possibly keep it. It's too precious. Thank you for letting me borrow it, Mrs. Nugent."

"You are very welcome, and we'll argue the rest out at a later time. Now let's get downstairs, and Riley and I will be honored to take you to meet the believers of our church."

Riley lined up their buggy with the rest that surrounded the church. He came around to help Mary and Beth down, and the three made their way to the white frame building.

Beth walked close to Mary. "Please don't leave me alone," she begged. "I wouldn't know what to do with myself."

"Don't worry; you are in safe hands." Mary straightened her hat with the lacy brim and a single white rosebud, and they made their way to the entrance of the church.

"We brought a beautiful visitor this morning, Pastor Thomas," said Riley as he shook hands with a man in a dark suit standing at the door. "This is Elizabeth Faraday."

The man looked at her oddly, and Beth decided he must know of her tomboy days. He smiled and greeted her with recognition. "We're happy you can be with us this morning, Miss Faraday. I remember you as a little girl, but now Mr. and Mrs. Nugent have brought us a grown-up young lady. I hope to see you here often."

They passed through the doorway, and inside Beth saw rows of long wooden benches that people had begun to fill. Children, some sleepy and some wide-eyed, occupied many of the spaces alongside the adults. In front of the benches stood an upright desk. Beth felt as wide-eyed as the children, curious about every detail and every person.

She saw many people with whom she did not have a friendly relationship. Finding herself an object of curiosity, she found it hard to be calm and aloof. She had vowed she'd be so.

Unsmiling, her gaze passed over the crowd as she tried to gain composure. Suddenly, across the aisle to her right, a pair of brown eyes looked steadily into hers. Sitting with his mother, who wore a pink summer dress, was the one and only Travis Warden. Beth looked away. At that same moment, Mortimer Warden brought in two flat brass bowls from a side room and set them on a table beside the door. Was the world populated with Wardens?

Apparently so, for Beth saw all the Warden relations enter, family by family. Each time a friendly acknowledgment swept the room. The relatives seemed genuinely glad to see each other, and later they seemed to enjoy the pleasure of being together even in silence. In Beth's mind, a new idea took hold.

As she listened to the sound of a melodic tune from a reed organ in front of the room to the left, Beth felt a similar warmth in the Nugents' closeness. A sense of community with the group welled in her heart, and waves of gratitude overcame all other emotions.

A quartet of singers gathered before the people and sang a song Beth had never heard before. It was heartily received, and afterward the flat brass bowls her father's employer had set on the side table were passed down each row of benches. Her own curiosity sparked Beth to watch the movement carefully. Were her eyes deceiving her? She had supposed the bowls held candy for restless tots, but she was wrong. The people were placing *money* in them! Even the children.

When the plate came to them, Riley Nugent put in more money than Beth had ever seen at one time. The bowls were being taken back to the side room before Beth got over her alarm. A glance at Mary brought a smile and a placating pat on her hand. It would be explained. Beth wondered what came next.

She hadn't long to wait. Pastor Thomas stood behind the tall desk in front and opened a big book. Then he read words from the page—words Beth knew she would never forget. "Come unto me, all ye that labour and are heavy laden, and I will give you rest." The pastor said those were words spoken by Jesus, the Son of God, in the part of the Book named Matthew.

Beth had read about Jesus in the books she borrowed, but she had never discussed that subject with anyone. Until Mary invited her to church, she'd given Jesus little thought.

The pastor talked on, introducing her to the Savior, and Beth was spellbound. The world around her fell away as the minister told how the cities Jesus spoke to had forsaken God. In prayer He thanked God for allowing His own humble children abundant blessings because they believed He and God were one. It was to people like her that Jesus had come. No matter how great their troubles or hers, if they or a seventeen-year-old girl believed in Jesus, He would give them rest all their lives.

She wanted Jesus as her friend: a friend who loved her despite her faults, a friend who would let her know she was not alone, a friend who loved her even though she was not rich or educated. She needed Jesus.

Stepping away from his stand, the pastor invited the people to give their hearts to Jesus Christ. Without looking back, Beth stood and went forward to receive that invitation. She felt Jesus beside her as she walked, and she was sure. No matter what came after, she was sure she had made the right choice.

⁂

The expression on Elizabeth Faraday's face puzzled Travis. Was she truly giving her heart to the Lord, or was she fooling the people, getting back at them for their out-of-the-ordinary treatment because of her father? Had she really changed? *Lizzy* had walked around trying to pick a fight ever since he'd known her. His mother said maybe it was because she was raised with two brothers and by a father who would rather drink than work. Regardless of the answer, Travis realized he hadn't spent a minute worrying or praying about her.

He'd been too busy making his own way in the world. He wanted God to show him what he should do, but so far he hadn't received an answer. He'd been in school in Baltimore, and now his sister and brother-in-law wanted him to come to Philadelphia to study. That path was cluttered with emotion. His future lay open before him like a huge, unanswered question.

He caught a glimpse of Elizabeth's happy face, so sure of what she was doing. Her joy had to be real.

Travis knew her background. Her mother died suddenly when she was eleven. Her father, Sid Faraday, was employed at the mills. His drinking kept the family poor. In the study one day, his father had spoken to him about the Faradays.

"I'm glad you're concerned, Travis. So am I," he said. "But there's only so much we can do. Sid is not a good workman. He's a lazy man who wants to blame his troubles on others. I keep him on because of the children. Fred's a good boy, and now that you've stopped irritating Elizabeth, she may grow up to be like her mother. Charlie, I don't know well. He likes his father's ways. So far, I don't hold out much hope."

"What's to be done, Father?"

"Pray for them. Before Carrie and Graham led us all to the Lord, I'd have thought that was a silly thing to say, but no more. God's Word says it over and over. Matthew 21:22 says, 'And all things, whatsoever ye shall ask in prayer, believing, ye shall receive.' God wants us to pray for the Faradays without question. He's given us a promise.

"I'll keep Sid on at the mills. Fred will have a job, too, as much as he can handle. If she'll let you, you might try to make friends with Elizabeth." His father got up from his desk and looked him in the eye. "Be kind to the family, Travis. Don't judge. Be kind like Jesus."

Travis remembered when his father was "Papa" to Carrie and to him—an unsaved papa. The Lord had turned his father's life around, and just as the pastor had said this morning, Christ had given him rest. The Lord had worked through Mortimer Warden to bring others to Himself, and a kinder, more just man did not exist. Travis was sure of it. Elizabeth's coming to Christ would make all the Wardens happy.

⁂

After the service many church members gathered around Beth to encourage her. She had never known such happiness. Everyone she spoke with seemed honestly glad for her. Only when the Wardens came forward did she feel nervous. This was Pa's and Fred's employer.

Mrs. Warden spoke first. "Elizabeth, we are so happy you've made this decision. We remember what it was like for us."

"Yes, we do. I know this will make a big difference to you." Mr. Warden leaned forward to whisper. "If we can ever help you in any way, please let us know."

Beth searched his face as he pulled away. He looked to be telling the truth. Was he being honest, or was Mr. Warden putting on an act? Pa didn't trust him. It was hard for her to do so when she had never heard a complimentary word about the man. As she hesitated, another voice came from behind her. This time it was his son, Travis.

"I'm glad you've accepted Jesus, Elizabeth. Faith in the Lord is the best choice you'll ever make. We'll be praying for you."

He went away then, but she kept hearing his words in her mind. Travis Warden would be praying for her? Did that mean he wouldn't be splashing muddy water on her, or calling her names, or looking down his nose at her? Small chance. He must not read the same Book Pastor Thomas did. She'd do a better job of serving the Lord than that!

The Wardens and the Nugents were conversing. When Mary caught Beth's eye, she excused herself to lead her to a tall, neatly dressed lady in a fashionable brown dress and hat.

"Elizabeth Faraday, this is my dear friend, Virgie Bower. As I'm sure you know, she's the Wardens' daughter. She has an idea that may interest you. And I also have an idea. Virgie, would you and Conrad accompany us to our home? We will have lunch, and afterward we three ladies can talk while the men enjoy a good visit." Mary's engaging smile promoted the idea.

Virgie glanced toward her husband, standing within earshot. "Mary, are you sure it's not an imposition? Conrad and I will be glad to take Elizabeth home, and we can talk on the way."

"No, no! I want to be in on the conversation, and Beth is staying for lunch."

"All right, if you're sure. We'll follow you."

Both carriages set off. Curious, Beth wondered if she would be as enthusiastic about Mrs. Bower's idea as Mary Nugent seemed to be.

❧

Later, after lunch, Virgie explained. "I have a good, dependable woman who cleans, a cook who is a jewel, and a lady who washes for me. So I have time on my hands." Virgie was almost apologetic, as it was known that her husband also came from a wealthy family. "I'd like to start a school for young ladies," she continued. "If you agree, Elizabeth, I'll start with you. Mary has told me how eager you are to learn and that you teach yourself by borrowing books."

The compliment and the offer overwhelmed Beth. She tried to speak, but words would not come. She merely listened.

"I would require you to do certain chores, such as sewing and tasks to beautify our home. Our activities should train you to keep your own home someday. I intend to educate you as we work. Now, since you'd be letting me experiment on you as my first class, I would pay you a pittance for your time."

Her ears rang. Beth thought she would faint from happiness. But could it be? She rose slowly from her chair in the Nugent parlor, a hand at her throat.

They'd had a delicious tea served in Mary's thin, delicate cups from an enchanting tea service Beth had so admired. But that was only the beginning. The room they occupied repeated the enchantment. The Nugents' concept of beauty with furniture and colors called out to Beth's soul. They were all God's gifts. From her present life of drudgery, she suddenly felt raised to a limitless future.

"I think you've stunned her, Virgie," murmured Mary.

"I hope not. From what you've told me, I think she and I will be good for each other. You know I've always wished I had a daughter. If she'll allow me to call her Beth, too, we'll become the best of friends, and I'll try to be a good teacher."

Beth turned to them. "You can't know what it means to have two such friends who believe in me and want to help me. I gave my life to Jesus, and He has given me so much; I don't know how to thank Him."

She seated herself again and faced Virgie across the tea table. "All I can do is tell you the truth. Nothing would make me happier than to say yes right now. But I don't know if Pa will even consider letting me accept your offer. There's so much work at home, and if it's not done," she said hoarsely, "I'll be in trouble."

Mary clasped Beth's hand. "We must pray. Nothing is impossible with God. We must expect Him to show us how to make this wonderful adventure happen. I think it would mean the world to you."

Nodding her head, Virgie held out her hand, too. "I'd like us to pray together. Shall we go to the Lord right now?"

Beth bowed her head as the others did, and she listened as both prayed for her. Her heart calmed as the women asked God to bless her with the education Virgie could give her. Books were a miracle to Beth, and she realized she could familiarize herself with the world through books Mrs. Bower owned or had access to. *Think of it!*

Despite His newness to her, Beth wanted to talk to Jesus, too. She had a particular request.

Please, Sir, forgive me if I don't pray as well as these ladies, but I need to ask a question. If I work for Mrs. Bower, will Travis Warden be around? She's his sister, so he must visit. I don't know how I can stand it if he's always looking over my shoulder. If You let me do this, would You please work it out so I'd never have to see him?

four

The post came, and on his morning ride, Travis caught the coach at the crossroads after he left the house.

"Mornin', Mr. Travis. Got some packages for your dad and a letter from Pennsylvania for you," said the leathery-skinned old carrier.

"Thank you, sir." Travis saluted him, traded a large grin for the letter and packages, and the carrier went on his way.

He dropped Hero's reins, put the packages in a saddlebag, and opened the letter from his sister Carrie. Most of it contained answers to questions he had asked in previous letters. The second page, however, was more interesting. Travis grinned. His sister addressed the paragraph with his name from childhood.

> *Trouble, Graham and I want you to come to Philadelphia this summer and visit the University of Pennsylvania. It's a fine school, and I'm sending Papa some printed material about it so he will be satisfied with the fees. If you decide to enroll, you might get in the fall session. I know we mentioned this before, but Graham and I want you to know how serious we are in our invitation. Just let me know when you can be here, and I'll have your room ready for you.*

Carrie added more to encourage him and stressed their concern for his future. He looked out over the surrounding landscape of rolling fields. Why not go? He could at least take a closer look. Maybe the trip would resolve his restlessness. God was in control of his life, but for some reason he was still casting around as if waiting for some colossal event that would set him on the right track. His faith seemed too shallow to wait for God to do what He had promised.

He stuck the letter in his inside coat pocket and picked up Hero's reins. White clouds scurried ahead of a rising wind, but he decided there was still time for a ride. There was no place he had to be, and soon he found himself nearing the Faraday place. Grimacing, he eyed the run-down dwelling.

Just as I thought. It's more of a hovel than I remember it. How do they stand to live here? How Elizabeth manages to keep house under these conditions is a wonder: the porch ready to fall off, bricks missing from the chimney, not near enough windows. She probably has to come outside to sew. And look at that yard. Three men in the family, and they can't cut the grass. They should be ashamed!

He was suddenly feeling sorry for the girl. With all she had to do, did they expect her to tend the yard? He noticed she had no flowers growing. She had no time for a simple, creative task that would bring her pleasure. He compared his own home, overlooking the little village. Regally situated on a low hill surrounded by shade trees and well-kept flower beds, it was the grandest house in the territory. Comparing the interiors of the two homes would be out of the question.

No wonder Elizabeth resented his presence in her life. Each incident that had occurred seemed an intrusion, defining her as an individual of lower value.

"What are *you* doing here?"

Neither Travis nor Hero had felt Beth's presence behind them, and both jerked to attention. He turned the horse toward her.

"I was out for my morning ride and just happened by," he said, wondering himself why it had taken place. "I assume there is no toll for using this private road."

Beth switched two books she carried to the other arm and

brushed at the cotton apron tied over her dark work dress. "No, that's the kind of thing a Warden would think of. Since the Faradays don't own the road, it wouldn't occur to us to charge travelers for using it." She rested a fist on her hip and waited for his reaction.

Travis took off his hat and controlled his temper. "Miss Faraday, uh. . .Elizabeth, can't we just talk without arguing? As long as I'm here, I'd like to say again how glad I am that you gave your heart to the Lord yesterday. In fact, my whole family was happy we were there to witness it," he finished breathlessly.

"At the time it happened, I wasn't thinking about your family. I'm well aware that our family is obligated to yours because of Pa's and Fred's jobs. But that doesn't mean I'd put on an act to make people think better of us. I really wanted to give my heart to Jesus."

Travis slid from the saddle and took a step closer. "Of course you did. No one fakes his salvation. If he did, it wouldn't mean a thing." He caught her quick glance. "I know how you felt. I remember when I came to the Lord."

Beth gasped. "You mean *you're* a believer?"

Her skeptical face shook Travis. "Well, if you can't tell I'm a Christian, I must not be doing a very good job of it."

Beth seemed to be the one shocked now, but she recovered quickly. "You have to admit that putting toads down my back and pushing me off the riverbank are two reasons I don't trust that statement. And making fun of my pa is a continuing joke with you."

"Lizzy, you'd have to prove that one." He shook his head. "I'm sorry, Elizabeth. I slipped."

"As long as you've slipped, I may as well tell you. I'd like to be called Beth instead of Elizabeth. Mary Nugent calls me Beth, and I think it suits me."

He smiled. "It does." His gloved hand tugged at Hero's

saddle. "I hear you and my sister Virgie are going to be spending time together."

"It isn't definite. Pa doesn't even know about the decision I made yesterday. When I get the courage to tell him, he may not let me work for Mrs. Bower. I've been praying some today, asking Jesus to help me tell him."

"Won't your brother help you? Fred, I mean. I doubt Charlie will be on your side."

Her temper flared again. "Travis Warden, you're on thin ice. My family may not mean much hereabouts, but they're *my* family, and I won't have you saying bad things against them! I should have known not to give you an inch!" She turned on her heel and marched the path to the house. At the porch she turned back. "If I do start working for Mrs. Bower, I hope I don't ever see you there!"

"Don't worry about that! I'm going to Philadelphia for a while. If things turn out as they might, I'll be moving there. Is that good enough?"

ᘐ

Beth trembled so that she could hardly navigate her way inside. Once there, sobs racked her body. She huddled in a chair and buried her face in an old stuffed pillow. It took several minutes to calm herself to the point where her mind could shed light on what had happened.

First, he had ridden past the house. Why? It was not his habit. He was dressed in his best: gray jacket, black riding breeches, blue ascot. His tall riding hat emphasized his slender physique, and the gray jacket fit his wide shoulders magnificently. His riding by so casually seemed curious.

But what followed had destroyed assets his appearance had simply fabricated.

"It's the same as always," she sobbed. "He couldn't wait to start a quarrel." Yet her conscience chided her. She had been first to lose her temper, and she was sorry. She truly wanted to obey the Lord and live in peace. Still, if Travis hadn't answered her so rudely, it wouldn't have happened.

Worst of all, she had shared things she hadn't meant to with one who had always been her enemy. Like her new name, Beth. Why had she told *him* of all people? She'd also said she hadn't told Pa about her salvation, and then he had lied about criticizing her father. Everyone knew the Wardens criticized Pa. It was all over town. But was that proof? She'd never heard it said out loud.

Beth dried her eyes. If she'd let him, he would have given his opinion about his sister's future attempts to educate her. She was glad she hadn't talked further on that subject.

Rising from the chair, she pulled a wicker laundry basket from under the washtub stand and carried it to the clothesline to bring in the clothes she'd washed. Inside, she sprinkled those she would iron, rolled them up, and packed them in the basket with a damp towel over them. She'd iron tomorrow.

Early that morning before it got hot, she'd gathered green beans from the small garden she kept, and she'd hoed out a few weeds while she was at it. Now she washed the beans, snapped them, and put them on to boil with chunks of bacon. Closer to suppertime, she'd add potatoes and make biscuits.

She was very tired, partly because of tension. She still had to confront her father on two counts, and she couldn't forget her scene with Travis Warden. Usually she could forget him, but today was different, and she didn't know why. Their conversation had done nothing but confuse her.

❧

"So you joined up with those Bible readers, eh?" her pa questioned that night. "There's a bunch of 'em at the mill. That's all they talked about today: 'Lizzy went to church yesterday. Lizzy went to church yesterday.' Said they guessed I'd be goin' with you before long. My gang nearly laughed their heads off."

Beth polished the plate she was drying until it shone like glass. She licked her dry lips. "I was going to tell you, Pa. I was afraid you'd be put out with me. I wanted to wait until the right time."

Sid slammed his chair back against the floor. "There ain't no 'right time' for news like that. How'll you get your work done with all this churchgoin'?"

"I'll just have to work harder, Pa."

"If she gets behind, I'll help out a little," Fred offered, his face reddening.

"Well, well, *Miss Faraday*," Sid mocked Fred in a feminine voice. "If you can get your housework done, can you come down to the mills and help out there a little?"

Listening from the old settee, Charlie nearly split his sides laughing; and Beth fired such a look at him that he sobered immediately.

"She works like a pack animal around here, Pa," Fred spat. "We oughta all be helping her more. Beth, I shoulda picked those beans for you and hoed the weeds. I could help out more. We all could, and it would only be right. We forget sometimes that you're only a little over five feet tall and not very stout."

Beth's look told him thanks, and she turned to the dishpan. The room went silent, and Beth faced them again. "You may as well know this, too. The Wardens' daughter, Mrs. Bower, has asked me to do a few extra things for her at her house, and she'll pay me a little for the chores I do. I won't be away from home very long at a time; and while I work, she'll teach me things like Miss Stimpson teaches the girls in her school."

Sid's anger rose. "So here's another Warden ready to take over. What you tryin' to do? Put 'em in charge of us? You'd think me workin' for the old man would be enough. Now you're in cahoots with the daughter. Fred, when she starts this, are you goin' to wash the dishes, too? Looks like our society lady won't have much time for her duties to us."

Before Fred could speak, Beth exclaimed, "Pa, can't you understand? I live in a world of housework and you men—nothing else. If Mrs. Nugent hadn't helped me, I wouldn't even know how to act in church. Since my sweet mother died, I haven't had any girlfriends except Clara Watts. She was a faithful friend. Only she made one mistake. She was born black, and according to you, she wasn't good enough to associate with me."

Her father wouldn't look at her. "Do what you want to!" he yelled, charging out the front door. "I don't care."

Beth and Fred traded glances. It was true. Their father didn't care what they did. He wouldn't be back to see if everything at his home was safe and in order that night. Only fathers with names like Nugent, Warden, and Bower did that.

≈

Beth didn't mind the long walk to the Bower home, but today a family going her way in a wagon picked her up. The Nugents and Bowers had let her route be known to the church members in case they could include it on their schedule of weekly errands. She had been up since five o'clock and had her work done by eight, so she was ready for a little rest in the back of the wagon.

The wagon stopped at the Bowers' gate. Beth hopped out, thanked the driver, and made her way to the front door. A border of pansies lined the pathway to a hedge of shrubbery around the stone house. No trees grew in the yard, but behind the house stood a forest that shaded the dwelling from the western sun.

Mrs. Bower greeted her cheerfully at her knock, and Beth enjoyed a luxury of riches for the eye as she followed the lady through her opulently appointed home. Completely opposite to the Nugent residence, sturdy dark woods combined with heavy fabrics and deep, varicolored carpets set the home in a class of its own. Its alternate style took Beth's breath away.

Their destination was a room where an open desk with a small stack of books and papers caught Beth's eye first. Then she saw them. Great cases of books covered two walls of the library, as her hostess called the room. A happiness she could hardly contain swept over her, and tears came to her eyes.

Mrs. Bower stepped close and put her arm around her shoulders. "What is it, dear? Why are you upset?"

Words didn't come easily. "I'm not upset, ma'am. It's just that. . .I didn't know there were this many books in the whole world. It's wonderful." Beth's gaze devoured the vast selection.

The older woman squeezed her shoulder. "They're yours to borrow, Elizabeth. Every last one of them." She pointed to the desk. "Here are some books I thought we might start with. I have some favorites, and we'll begin with those. There's sewing we must do, so we will take the books to the sewing room and take turns reading while we work. I've prepared questions for discussion when we read our selection for today. How does that sound? Does my schedule agree with you?"

Beth couldn't answer. Such an abundance of kindness and generosity was foreign to her. She swiped at her eyes for a moment. "Thank you, Mrs. Bower. I've never—"

Her hostess stopped her with a laugh. "I think we'd better come to an understanding. As long as we'll be seeing each other several times a week, why don't you call me Virgie? My real name is Virginia Mae, but, like you, I like being called by my nickname. So I'll call you Beth, and you call me Virgie." She approached a tall cabinet, opened the doors, and took out a flat box. "Now that's settled. Let's begin."

From the box, Virgie took out a long white strip of fine cotton material. "We'll start with a pair of pillowcases. We'll measure the length I need, then pull a horizontal thread and a vertical one to make the pieces absolutely square. That's where we'll cut. Then we sew the bottoms and the opposite sides to the folds. Is that the way you do yours?"

Warmth lit Beth's face, and she wondered how many times she'd blush while she was learning. "No, ma'am. I just cut them and sew them up. My biggest problem has always been finding time to make them when we need them."

Virgie obviously saw the opportunity for her first lesson in homemaking. "But have you thought how much easier they would be to iron if they were perfectly straight? Don't forget, we want designs and lace on them."

"Really? How nice! Mrs. Nugent has pillowcases like that. I saw them hanging on her clothesline one day. I want to do that. In a house as nice as this, you should have the prettiest pillows that can be made. How can I help?"

એ

"She's exactly the one I've been looking for, Mother. My hands don't work as well as they used to. Beth's going to be an enormous help," Virgie said.

Mrs. Warden smiled and placed the last sausage cake in the skillet with the others. "I'm glad, dear. That girl has always fascinated me. She seems so out of place in that family. Her mother was a sweet lady, but her father cut his own potential when he started drinking. I've often wondered how Lizzy fares with so much responsibility and a bitter, indolent father."

"I talked to her the other day at her home." Travis sauntered by the cook table and stabbed a pickled beet on a lettuce plate. "She still hates me," he said as if answering an unasked question.

Virgie turned the fried potatoes she had started. "Tell the young man to wait for supper, Mother. After all, it's his farewell supper." Giving her younger brother a playful leer, she said, "May I inquire as to the reason for your visit to Miss Faraday?"

"Simply riding by, Virgie. I tried to encourage her on her decision to accept the Lord. And of course we quarreled instead," he said, finishing the beet. Then he swallowed and stood straight, remembering. "She said she hoped she'd never see me at your house, and I told her she didn't have to worry about that for a while. I was leaving. And then I rode off."

As she tended the sausage, Gwendolyn listened to their conversation without interrupting.

"Is that some of the new sausage, Mother?" Travis asked, giving her a little hug. "Smells like it's seasoned just right."

"I think so, too." She fended off his attempt to fork a sausage. "It's not done yet, *Trouble*." He grinned at the tiny insult and kissed her forehead. His mother looked up into his face. "Now that she's helping Virgie, why don't you try to quarrel a little less with Lizzy? I think we owe that courtesy to the memory of her mother. Virgie says Beth's a wonderful helper, and she thinks she can do a lot for her."

"With both of you ready to box my ears, I think I'll go up and change." At the wide door to the dining room, he shook his finger at Virgie and let go a final salvo. "You're going to miss me when I'm away in Philadelphia."

As he turned the corner, chuckling, he heard Virgie and his mother giggling like schoolgirls.

five

With impassioned words from his parents still fresh in his mind, Travis caught a ride to Baltimore on the morning coach. The three had grouped in the parlor at dawn for a final talk.

"Are you sure this is what you want to do, Son?" Obviously at odds with the prospect of his son's plan to locate so far away, a frown creased Mortimer's forehead.

"I'm not sure what God wants me to do yet, Father, but I have to see for myself if this offer is from Him."

Gwendolyn, in her rocker, had not spoken. But then she stood and put her arms around her tall son. "I will pray that you'll get a clear picture of what the Lord wants from you, my son. You know we'll support you in whatever you decide." Her voice had lost the confidence with which she started.

"Now, Mother, we promised ourselves we'd be objective about this," cautioned Mortimer. "Travis came to us and stated frankly that he wanted to make inquiries at the University of Pennsylvania. The school has a good reputation, and with Carrie and Graham living in Philadelphia, we'd be foolish not to let him investigate the possibility."

Travis hugged his mother close. "After I'm gone, you'll think better of this. I don't know if the university is where I want to go; but I have to find out, or I'll always wonder if I made the right choice."

"Your mother will be all right," said his father softly. "I'll spend some time with her today. But she's strong. She'll adjust. You go on and stop feeling guilty." He pulled the chain on his pocket watch and opened the face cover. "It's time to get moving if you want to make that coach."

&

Travis traveled up the Chesapeake to stay overnight at the Maltby House in Baltimore. A day later he went through the Chesapeake-Delaware Canal and took another boat up the Delaware River to Philadelphia. To his surprise, Carrie and Graham were on hand to meet him at the landing.

Smiling, they rushed toward him, and Carrie threw herself into his arms. "Travis! It's so good to see you! How are Mama and Papa and Virgie and Caleb and Joshua? And all their husbands and wives? I mean—Oh! I'm so excited to see you, I don't know what I mean!"

Graham laughed, shook Travis's hand, and cuddled his wife close with his arm. "She could hardly wait for you to get here. She had me check every possible boat docking this week on the off chance that we could meet you."

Laughing, too, Travis exclaimed, "Thank you, Graham. I'm sure you're far too busy to carry out such a chore, but I have to admit, I'm glad you're here." His gaze passed over the waterfront, where dozens of people were occupied with passengers or cargo. "What a mob! Where do all these people come from?" he questioned in amazement.

"From everywhere," replied Carrie. "Travis, it's the most exciting city in the world! That's why I want you here. When you see the university, it will convince you that Philadelphia is where you should live. Come on! Let's go home." Slipping her arm through Graham's, she grabbed Travis's hand, and giggling, she pulled them along to the street to board an omnibus. Travis hardly had time to grab his valise.

Graham went back to Nugent & Nugent, the law office of Graham and his uncle Fredrick. Carrie saw him off with a kiss, then set up Travis at the kitchen table with a piece of cake and a cup of coffee. After answering at least a hundred questions, he called a halt.

"Can you go with me to the university as a guide, or should I draw up a map of the place?"

"I was in hopes you'd ask me." She sat in the next chair and pulled it close. "But I want it clearly understood: I will be perfectly content to wait as long as it takes when you have a chance to talk to an instructor face-to-face. I know how businessmen are—that is, except for Graham. It's not their style to have to put up with a *lowly* woman." The disdain in Carrie's voice needed no explanation.

"I understand, but unless you've other duties, I'd like you with me on this visit as much as possible. I've missed you." He reached for her hand and held it a moment.

"Me, too," she murmured, smiling. "Now I have a question. I know you love the Lord. You always have. But are you totally committed to the ministry, Travis?"

"That's what I've had in mind all along. Right now I'm waiting for the Lord to settle it, and I'm praying for patience. Why do you ask?"

"Mama told me how you helped the doctor when the Brighams' house burned last year, and it made me remember how well you cleaned and bandaged Clara Watts's leg when she got caught by the mower. It was a deep cut, but it left only a tiny scar because you knew what to do."

"So?" Travis spread his hands, palms up. "What's the point?"

"Have you thought of medicine as a career? I've often wondered if God gave you your tenderness with people as a talent for healing. The university has a wonderful medical school."

"Elizabeth Faraday would totally disagree with you about my tenderness. She thinks I'm the hardest-hearted man in the world," he jeered as he looked away.

"What's this? Something I don't know about?" Beneath Carrie's golden red, upswept hair, her brown eyes probed for answers to her questions.

With a wave of his hand, he tried to dismiss the subject. "No, no. I shouldn't have mentioned it."

She swatted his arm. "Now don't leave me out. Talk! I want to hear."

"We're talking about a seventeen-year-old girl, Carrie."

"I see. So much younger than you, eh?"

"Do you want to hear this or not?"

Carrie sat back and folded her hands in her lap. "I want to hear."

"You probably don't remember," said Travis, "but Beth and I never got along."

Giggling, Carrie inhaled a breath and blew it out. "Never got along? You two were the village nightmare. I can't imagine you even mentioning Lizzy's name."

"You're behind the times. We don't call her Lizzy anymore. She left that name to become Elizabeth. Then your mother-in-law called her Beth, and that's the name she likes now."

"How did Mary get into it?"

Bit by bit, he brought her up to date: the progression of Mary's friendship, Beth's salvation, Virgie's help, and Beth's eager attempt to learn. He sighed. "Virgie likes her. It's working out well at her house. Beth's her experiment in the start of a school for girls."

"But what about her family? I know she had a few problems at home."

"Sid's still as mean as ever. Still drinks. Fred's fifteen and has turned out to be a good, polite kid. We give him as much work at the mills as we can, but they're still poor. They don't just give away those jugs."

"Poor Lizzy—Beth. Does she like you underneath it all?"

"I doubt it. . . . I mean, what do I care? Her life is so complicated only God can straighten it out."

Carrie leaned forward. "I hear He's good at that, Travis. Lots of us depend on Him to get our lives straight." She sobered suddenly and looked away. "Graham and I have no children yet."

Travis knew better than to comment. Instead, he threw out an inane question. "Do you think Beth's too young for me?"

His sister stood and chuckled softly. "No. After the life she's had, she probably thinks she's a little too old for you."

&

The University of Pennsylvania was over a hundred years old. Travis and Carrie arrived at the school early, and he arranged for two appointments with instructors. She left him then to meet Graham.

The aging campus had a dramatic effect on Travis. What a rich piece of America's history he was seeing! Graham had awakened his patriotism in a discussion of politics after supper the night before. He had no idea when it would happen, but he was sure that, in time, his brother-in-law would run for political office. Graham was an energetic citizen who cared about his country.

Travis happened onto a gathering of medical students outside and found a seat nearby to listen. With the introduction of an intriguing subject, his curiosity drew him into the group. The students were eager to convert a potential doctor to their way of thinking, and rival opinions convinced Travis those kinds of give-and-take discussions were what he had been looking for. He felt God's first call to consider medicine as a profession, and he began to pray for the answer.

His appointments brought further encouragement to study at the university. The fact that the medical school cohabited with an institution of higher learning was a unique mark of distinction. He had to consider the school. Three of the students he'd met earlier managed to get permission for him to observe their classes the next day. Travis was delighted.

Early the next morning, he met the first of the students with whom he was slated to visit a class, and the routine continued until late in the day. He hadn't foreseen how intriguing the procedure would be. The teaching doctors' devotion to healing, plus their ability to explain their conclusions and opinions, impressed Travis as nothing ever had. In Baltimore he'd read medical books because they interested him, but he'd had no mentor and no instruction. Sitting in with the medical students, pieces of the puzzle came together, and his previous studies didn't compare.

He left his companions and found a chapel where he could have quiet time alone. Within its hallowed walls, he found a secluded spot, and he dropped to his knees and had a long talk with the Lord. His call to the medical field became clear.

The week ended with worship at Carrie and Graham's church, where Travis witnessed the active participation of his sister and her husband. He thought of his parents. How satisfied they would be to hear that the Nugents were stronger than ever in their faith.

❧

Monday morning brought his departure, and though he was sad to leave Philadelphia, somehow his return home brought a tinge of excitement. The decision to enter medical school had freed him from the turmoil with which he had wrestled for two years. At first his parents might be puzzled, but then they would accept his choice. If he meant to move to Philadelphia in the fall, the rest of the summer called for tying up loose ends in his personal life.

As the boat rocked steadily along the Elk River, Travis watched the shore slide past while reliving the week with the Nugents in Philadelphia. He liked the city. There was a lot going on. If he moved, he could leave the mills and their problems behind. The supposition left him startled.

What problems? His father handled his business with skill. Since he'd become a believer, he was a pillar in his church and respected and loved by the community. No, that was not true. Sid Faraday hated him. Beth Faraday's father hated Mortimer Warden.

Faraday remembered Mortimer's cutthroat business practices before his employer came to the Lord, and he'd never forgiven him. Time after time in the years since, he had been called in for drinking on the job and for careless mistakes that cost the vast grain mills money. He seemed to dare Mortimer to fire him. His father had been more than patient, and Travis wondered if Beth ever knew the truth of those incidents.

He pictured Beth in his mind and was startled again at the tug at his heart. Virgie had exposed her to a finer life than she knew existed, and she had access to literature beyond her imagination. But what about her home life? She was keeping house for her family plus helping Virgie. Was she receiving any consideration? Surely the men and Charlie took up some of the slack. Beth's pay from Virgie was generous.

Even with the extra work, Beth continued to keep an immaculate appearance. Her clothes were old and patched, but they were clean, and her fresh scent lingered indefinitely. It's what had drawn him to her when he'd ridden by her house. Her fair image lingered. Travis wondered how that long blond hair would feel, loosened from its braid and crushed in his hand.

Jolted from his daydream by a flight of seagulls, he looked left and right to see if anyone had detected his glide into fantasy. A glance at his red face would be all they needed, he supposed.

⁂

Travis retrieved Hero from the livery stable and started for home. Did he have enough time to check on the Faraday place? No, that was foolish. There was no reason to do such a thing. Nothing had changed in a week. Nevertheless, in the remaining twilight, he found himself on the road leading to Beth's home.

Ahead, a figure walked unsteadily along the edge of the road, and Travis slowed Hero's gait to learn its identity. At first he thought his eyes were deceiving him, but as he rode closer, there was no doubt. It was Beth. She was walking very slowly.

"Beth! What are you doing on the road? Are you just getting home from Virgie's?"

"Yes," she said wearily. "Some days there's more to do. Virgie's expecting company."

"Let me help you then." He swung out of the saddle. "Put your foot in my hands and sit in the saddle. I'll climb up behind and take you home. I can see how tired you are."

Beth panicked. "Oh no! I can't do that. Pa would have a tantrum!"

"Then let me take you partway," he said, caught by her fatigue. "Your father won't even know I'm around."

Beth backed away. "I don't think so. No. I'd better not."

Travis could see her exhaustion winning. He caught her hand. "Please, Beth. Don't walk. Ride with me."

He felt her hand relax, and with her foot in his clasped hands, he lifted her into Hero's saddle. When they were three-quarters of the way to her house, he gently let her down, and she ran the rest of the way.

❧

Virgie's day had called for a more strenuous chore than Beth had been assigned before. Because of the guests from New York, Virgie decided to rewash all the china to be used. To avoid breakage, she called on Beth because rheumatism had attacked the housekeeper. As usual, Beth had started her day at five o'clock. By the time the dishes were carefully washed and dried and stacked in their cabinets again, she was longing for home. Fairly compensating her for the extra work, Virgie had also slipped into Beth's reticule a length of the white cotton and a yard of red ribbon for her hair.

The men were on the porch when Beth got home, and her delay had given Sid time to imbibe.

"Don't you worry; I'll find out what's goin' on up there."

"Where, Pa?" she asked.

"At my old friend Mortimer Warden's house."

At once Beth came to attention. "What do you mean? What's happened?"

Her father thrived from attention focused on him. "I don't know what it is, but something funny's goin' on," Sid said importantly. "I'll find out what it is. You can count on it."

"Pa, maybe it would be better to stay away from the Wardens. You want to keep your job." As soon as she said it, she knew it was a mistake.

"And who do you think you're talking to? I'm the boss here. I'll do whatever I want to, and I won't ask you." Sid had forgotten the way the conversation started.

Beth spoke to smooth over what she'd said. "I'm sorry, Pa. I didn't mean to make you mad."

"You oughta be. Where's the supper? Nothin' fixed, and my stomach's rubbin' my backbone. Get in there and start cookin' so we can eat." Sid shuffled away, slumped in his porch chair, and promptly fell asleep.

Beth was grateful. She wanted to think about what he had said and what he meant. Her father would do anything to cause trouble for Mr. Warden. Maybe she could find out what he was planning.

Fred apologized to Beth for their father's mood and added, "I would have started supper if I'd known what to fix, but he was so mad, I figured I'd do more harm than good."

"It's all right, Fred. I'll hurry," she said and slipped inside.

Charlie threw a rock at the sound of an owl and growled, "You better hurry. We're hungry."

"Be quiet, Charlie," said Fred. "Can't you see she's tired? She must have had a lot to do, and she's not through yet."

"It's not my fault. I didn't ask her to go over there to work."

"But you don't mind what she brings home, either. You wait and see, Charlie. Someday you're going to be sorry you talked to her the way you have. Elizabeth's going to be a great lady, and you'll come to wish you'd treated her better."

Charlie snickered. "I won't hold my breath."

Though Charlie hurt her feelings, Beth didn't interrupt or let them know she was standing inside the door listening. She turned and went out the back to fetch wood for the stove.

&

Travis could still feel the warmth of Beth in his arms on the ride home. They hadn't talked on the way, yet he felt there was the beginning of a truce between them. Would it be permanent, or would it be broken when Beth wasn't scared anymore? Scared or not, the girl he'd held so briefly was a different Beth than the one he'd known as a child. Her womanly manner told him she was every inch a lady.

He didn't know how he felt about her. He'd talked to his sister about her because he had to talk to someone—and because their strong sibling bond was still there. His mother and Virgie may have wondered at the flippant way he'd mentioned Beth before he left for Philadelphia, but it was unlikely they'd remember it now.

"Lord," he prayed aloud, "I commit my way to You again. Help me do only Your will as You straighten the path I'm to follow. Help me face my parents and tell them what I plan to do, for I want to serve You with healing hands, Lord.

"For Beth's sake, I'd like to find a way to help the Faradays.

Take care of her, Jesus, and let one special person bring Sid to Your throne of grace. Only You can get him out of his alcohol trap, Lord. He needs You. Please help him."

six

After praying for Beth's problems, Travis opened his eyes. Hero was dependable. They were still homeward bound as if nothing world-shattering had happened. The house was just up the hill. He relaxed and shifted his weight on the horse, but he stopped abruptly.

For the second time that night, he saw a figure in shadow. This time, the figure heading to an unused outbuilding near the barn was a man, not a woman. A quarter moon was on the rise, and in the semidarkness, enough light shone to tell Travis the man knew exactly where he was going.

Travis spotted a line of light from the kitchen door, and in a moment, the portly frame of his father moved stealthily out into the night. Trees in the yard darkened the view, yet Travis was sure Mortimer's destination was the same outbuilding. He was right. A moment later, his father slipped inside. Stepping from the saddle, Travis tied Hero to a tree and watched.

What was happening? Why had his father not taken a lantern, and why was he meeting someone in a storage shed that had stood empty for years?

He waited, trying to make sense of it. Finally a decision came. This was not an ordinary thing. It was secret. In his heart, he knew what was happening. His father was a devout believer who felt God's presence in all things. Any clandestine activity was a result of prayer, or his father would not take part. Travis decided whatever the situation, he was Mortimer Warden's son. If danger was involved, he must be at his father's side. *Now.*

Casting a glance in all directions, Travis made his way from shadow to shadow, taking it slowly, watching for any intruder from the road or from the house. On the far side of the shed, a chute used to move grain once offered entry. He worked his way around to it. It was still there.

He scrambled quickly to an eyehole position and peered into the shack. It took some minutes for his eyes to accustom themselves to the darkness, but little by little he was able to make out the stout figure of his father. A single pinpoint of light shone from an unidentifiable source. Across from his father sat a man whose face he could not see, and he did not recognize the voice.

The man stood, and the two passed from sight to the door, which Travis barely heard open. A shuffling of feet came next, and running footfalls of his father's visitor advanced swiftly into the darkness. Travis rounded the building and met his father when he turned.

"Father—"

"Travis, is that you?" Mortimer stepped close to his son. "Don't say anything. Not a word. Come with me quietly."

Travis thought it extraordinary that a man of his father's size could cover the route back to the house with such silent grace. When they reached the back door, Mortimer gripped his arm and pointed to the kitchen stairs. Travis followed soundlessly, and he realized they were headed for the attic.

Once there, the two found seats on a packing case and a crate. The older man fought to catch his breath after the long climb. Travis reached out to pat him gently on the back.

"You always do the right thing, Papa. I should have known. He was a black man, wasn't he?"

Still panting, his father nodded. He had trouble talking, and Travis silenced him with a motion of his hand. But his father wouldn't be hushed.

"It won't wait, Son. I need to get back downstairs, and so do you. Hero's out there someplace. You have to get back down and come in the front as if you've just come home. Where are your belongings?"

"My valise is in town, at Virgie's. Conrad met my boat. Now stop trying to work out all the problems, and take time to get your breath. When you do, I think we've got more important matters to talk about than my valise."

Mortimer took off his vest and laid it aside. Travis noticed beads of perspiration on his father's forehead before he swiped them away with his handkerchief. He had no business engaging in such dangerous business. It was a job for younger men. No one should attempt such a venture at his age.

"Can you talk now, sir? I've got to know."

"It's a long story." Mortimer rested his arm along the back of a discarded desk chair and took a few deep breaths. "After I came to the Lord, He dealt with me in a way I never expected. I thought of all those I had done wrong with my bad temper and demanding ways, and I became so ashamed, I could hardly look anyone straight in the face. Then one day out on the bay, I witnessed a slave being mistreated on a boat that had come in from Mississippi.

"With crews made up of both white men and a few Negroes, now and then it is possible for a slave to slip through to the North undetected. This man didn't. His master had found him. He nearly beat the man to death before my eyes. I vowed to God that I'd help one of those poor people escape to freedom. The trouble is, there's no end to it."

His father's frustration startled Travis. "No, Father, you can stop it. It's dangerous to your health! I can see what it does to you. Let someone who's younger take on the responsibility. There are other sympathizers in the village."

Mortimer's look made him feel as if he were ten years old again. "How little you understand, Travis. We're not talking about one or two people, Son. We're talking about thousands. People who didn't ask to come to this country in the first place and are begging for freedom to live the normal lives we take for granted. When I said, 'there's no end to it,' I meant there are hundreds in the South depending on those of us who care enough to help them to a humane life. I *have* to do this."

Travis could see he did. "How long have you been a conductor on the Underground Railroad, Father?"

"I see you are familiar with the term. Our place has been a station for several years. And I've never regretted a day of it. I looked into the eyes of that man on the boat that day, and I knew no one should have to stand such treatment. As a believer, I couldn't stand by and do nothing. Tonight's man left here with food and dry clothing. A fishing boat will take him to Bodkin Point. Then he'll slip away to Baltimore and beyond, perhaps to Canada. I believe the Lord has connected me with those I needed to know, and He has used me to save lives—many Christian lives."

At a loss for words, Travis simply stared at his father. He had always loved him, even when intimidated by him, but never had he admired him so much as now.

❧

Mary was weeding a flower bed in the front yard when Beth opened her front gate the next morning.

"Company! I'm delighted." Seeing Beth's fatigue, she laid aside her gloves and pushed back her wide-brimmed hat. "You're just in time for some iced tea. New ice at the icehouse. Aren't we blessed? A boat came in yesterday."

Beth smiled but said nothing. She was too tired even for the conversation she so desired.

"Beth, are you ill?"

"No, just tired." She sauntered toward the front stoop to sit down. "I wanted to talk to you."

"Let's go inside then." Mary picked up her gloves and led the way inside to the kitchen.

She asked Beth to take a seat while she washed her hands, and then she chipped ice into a bowl from a block in the icebox. It was soon crackling in their tall glasses of tea. Mary invited Beth to follow her into her sitting room for their talk. In seconds, Beth was ready to share her troubles with her friend.

"I need prayer, Mary."

Her friend propped an elbow on the chair arm to listen.

"My life is changing, and I'm confused. Virgie is very good to me. She has taught me things about sewing and cooking that I didn't know, and she discusses with me in detail what we read. I'm learning so much.

"But Pa is mad at me half the time, and he talks meaner and meaner. It's like he's jealous. They don't help me at home, not even bringing in the wood to cook. Fred wants to, but Pa won't let him. Pa talks mean to him, too, and I'm afraid Fred may try to run away." She sighed and clasped her hands in her lap. "So much trouble."

Mary sipped her tea and touched her lips with her napkin. "Beth, you told me how much the verse meant to you that Pastor Thomas quoted the day you became a believer: Matthew 11:28. 'Come unto me, all ye that labour and are heavy laden, and I will give you rest.' It's a promise, dear. God will see you through this and give you blessings you've never dreamed of.

"Let's leave Fred's problem to the Lord for right now. Pray about it. God may have the answer sooner than we think. Now, about your work with Virgie. Are you so tired because she's working you harder than she agreed to in the beginning?"

"No. It's because I have so much more work at home. Yesterday was a long day at Virgie's, but I won't be going back while her guests are here, so things will be easier."

"Have you saved enough to buy some material for a new dress?"

"Oh, no, Mary. Pa needs what Virgie gives me. He says prices are going up all the time, and he has obligations I don't know about."

Beth wondered if Mary was feeling well. Her face had turned pale, and she seemed very distressed. She hoped she hadn't said anything out of place. Maybe she shouldn't speak later of the more personal question on her mind.

"The Lord has the answers to these troubles, Beth. Let's wait on Him. I'm not putting you off, dear. *I'm* the one who needs a little time. I'd like to think and pray about what you've told me."

Beth took her hand. "Mary, you told me once that I could speak to you about anything I wanted to. All I had to do was ask."

Evidently the reminder was a calming potion to Mary. The color in her face became normal. Smiling slightly, she said, "Yes. Do go on, Beth. I want to hear."

"I'm not sure, but I think there's a boy. . .I mean, almost a man, who. . .maybe. . .uh, *maybe* likes me."

Mary smiled again. "I'm not surprised, dear. In fact, I'd be more surprised to find it untrue. You're a very pretty girl, Beth."

Beth squirmed in her chair and at last found her voice. "But it might surprise you to know who, *whom*, I think it is."

"Then surprise me. Please?" Mary's gaze locked on Beth's.

"Travis Warden."

Serene little Mary chortled and clapped her hand over her mouth. Control was not to be found. She threw back her head and let go laughter that could be heard clear to Delaware.

❧

It was a brand-new dress—not just borrowed. One that had never been worn. Beth had repeated all of Sid's objections to charity, but Virgie had a mind of her own. The week progressed, and she had worked on her project while enlightening Beth in the archaic English of William Shakespeare's *The Merchant of Venice*.

When Beth tore herself away to go home, Virgie shared her surprise with the girl. "The garment I've been working on since our friends went home is a Sunday dress for you. I think it should be ready for you to wear to church this Sunday."

"I told you, Virgie, it's out of the question. Pa won't—"

"I've worked out a plan. I'm going to take you home in the buggy today, and I'm going to sit right there and talk to that man myself."

"You can't, Virgie. He'd be rude to you. You don't realize how mean he can be. He may even be. . .he may not be, uh, himself," she said as gently as she could.

"I know how he can be, Beth. The whole town knows," said Virgie, verifying what Mary Nugent had said early in their acquaintance. "It's time he knows that not everyone approves."

So fearful was Beth that when the servant brought the buggy around, she could hardly climb into the conveyance on her trembling legs. On the road, she and Virgie did not converse at all. Beth prayed the whole way.

At home she flew into her preparations for supper. Soon the fire she had laid was flaming in the iron stove. The rest went quickly, and the meal would be ready. No more than an hour later, Sid and Fred came, Sid walking steadily, Beth noticed. Virgie's presence, however, secured a deadly look from her father, and Beth's trembling began again.

"Mr. Faraday," announced Virgie, "you and I need to have a frank talk. I've made a dress for Beth to wear to church. I understand you don't welcome what you consider charity, and I suppose you would categorize the dress I made as charity."

Auburn-haired Virgie pulled herself up to her full height of five and a half feet and with a grim expression faced Sid. "I call it a gift to a sweet young lady who has helped me immeasurably in the last few weeks. Everyone likes Elizabeth; and if you drank less, the town would forgive and like you, too. You are the head of a family, sir."

Sid seemed taken aback for the moment. "Well—"

"I'm not asking your permission to give the dress to Beth, and I'm not asking if you will let her go to church without harassing her. What I am telling you is this: You work for my father. So does Fred. Not once have I ever interfered in my father's business, but if you don't start treating Elizabeth fairly and letting her live a more normal life, I will insist that my father let you go at the mills."

Sid snorted and turned his head, smirking. "And you're supposed to be such a good Christian. All you Wardens are such good Christians, aren't you?"

"We try to be, yes. Yet I believe when you see unfair things happening to someone you love, you should try to help." She picked up her handbag and smoothed her gloves. "I'm going now. But I'm warning you that if I can help this child in any way, I will. Let it happen, Sid Faraday. Just let it happen."

Beth thought Virgie looked like a queen, regally dismissing her court by leaving the room.

❧

Still in the throes of forbidden knowledge of his father's station on the Underground Railroad, Travis had thought of little else since he got home from Philadelphia. So far, nothing had been said about his decision to study medicine. He had to decide when to break the news.

Congress had passed a strict fugitive slave law in 1850. Slaves and those who helped them escape from their owners could suffer dire consequences. Large fines and imprisonment were a possibility. He doubted his mother knew of his father's illegal activity. She was far too delicate to receive such rash information. She might suffer heart palpitations as she had when he was a child. His father had protected all of them.

He was still thinking of the chaos that was a heartbeat away when he fastened Hero's reins to a hitching post at the side of the church. His parents followed in their carriage, and when they stopped some distance away, he hurried to the vehicle to help his mother down. But Gwendolyn grabbed the side of the door when Travis missed her hand, and she nearly fell.

"Son! What are you doing?" she cried.

Travis tore his eyes from Beth, who was getting out of the Nugents' buggy, and apologized, his face glowing red. "Mother, I'm sorry! I don't know what came over me. Are you hurt?"

"No thanks to you, young man. I thought you reached out your hand."

"I did. I, uh, became distracted."

His mother laughed shortly when she followed the focus of his gaze. "Oh, now I see. You wished you were helping *her* out instead of me." She giggled and patted his face, which still glowed crimson.

Mortimer came around to them. "What are you up to? Did I miss something?"

A soft chuckle rose from Gwendolyn's throat. "Look around you, Mortimer. That beautiful girl in the blue dress almost cost me a fall from the carriage. My son said he was 'distracted.'"

Mortimer turned. "Well, I say! Travis, no wonder you were distracted. Elizabeth certainly looks pretty."

She did. Travis thought he had never seen anyone so beautiful. The blue dress his sister had made for her fell in deep folds from her tiny waist, and around her neck lay a collar of white pleats. Beth's blond hair tumbled loosely around her shoulders, shining with the brightness of the sun. The focus of her blue eyes roamed the groups of arrivals until it finally settled on him, and she smiled. Travis felt the familiar tug at his heart and knew that nothing in the world compared with the likes of Beth Faraday when she smiled.

"Well, let's get in, Son. This is still the Lord's day."

❧

Beth felt her face warm, and she turned quickly to Mary Nugent. In a show of joviality, Riley held out both arms to escort the two ladies to the church entry. Inside, they took their usual seats on the third row of the benches; and from the corner of her eye, Beth watched the tall, broad-shouldered enemy of her youth follow his parents into the same row to their right. Her thoughts turned to what had happened outside the church.

Mary and Riley had seen the little tableau between Travis and herself, and she doubted they were more surprised than she. How many others had seen? She tried to make herself smaller, to settle back onto the bench out of view.

Seated forward to her left, Virgie caught her glance and approved her appearance with a smile and a nod. Beth felt she should be sitting straight and tall to show off her friend's generous gift. Try as she might, her courage failed her. She might have on the world's prettiest dress, but she was still a lowly Faraday.

❧

"It's Monday, Gwendolyn. Don't look for me early." Mortimer took a last bite of hot biscuit slathered with butter. "Are you ready, Travis?"

"Ready." Travis gave his mother a hug.

"Travis?" she said.

Pressing his hands down his coat to smooth it and giving his hat a last touch, Travis turned at the sound of his mother's plaintive voice. "Yes, Mother?"

"I hope this goes well this morning. I'll be praying for you to have the right words."

"Thank you, Mother. I'm sure it will work out. I appreciate Father's attitude. He always wants the best for everyone."

"I'll see you tonight."

Travis winked, smiling at her, and he hurried to catch up with Mortimer. The horse and buggy were waiting, and his father had climbed into the passenger side. Travis soon had the horse on the road.

At the mills, Mortimer made for his office, and Travis looked on the gristmill floor for Fred Faraday. He spotted him almost at once.

"Fred, could you spare a minute?" he called.

"Sure, Mr. Travis," he said, grunting as he slid a heavy sack of grain off his shoulder.

"Do you know Mr. Riley Nugent, whose shop makes the beautiful furniture?"

"Sure, sir," he said, swiping his cap from his head. "He makes some mighty nice things."

"Riley and I talked at church yesterday, and he would like you to work for him."

Trying to find words, a choking sound erupted from Fred's throat. "Wh–what?" he muttered.

Travis grinned. "He'd like you to come to work for him. He will train you to learn the business."

"You mean he'll teach me to make furniture?" Fred whispered.

Travis looked back over his shoulder. Sid Faraday had entered the room, and the effect was immediate.

"I appreciate him asking, but I'll have to talk it over with my pa." Fred could hardly speak for watching his father.

Travis realized he should have arranged to meet the boy away from the mills, but that wasn't possible now. A tyrant like Sid Faraday would insist on approving the change of employment, even if it were to Fred's advantage. He'd simply confront Sid.

"Mr. Faraday!" he exclaimed.

"Yeah?" Sid sauntered across the floor and slouched to a halt.

"Riley Nugent has authorized me to offer Fred a job that may mean a good future if he works hard. We thought if I came here and made it clear there are no hard feelings if he changes jobs, he could start right away. What do you say, Fred? Are you ready to start?"

Fred's wide smile said yes, but his look traveled to his father, and he murmured, "What about it, Pa? Is it all right with you?"

"Of course it's all right with him!" Travis interrupted. "What father wouldn't want his son to get ahead? You'll be learning a good trade. You might even start your own business someday. Think of that!"

Fred clasped Travis's hand in happiness. "Then I'm ready to start! Tell Mr. Nugent I'll be there early tomorrow morning."

They shook hands, and Travis left, satisfied that his plan had been successful. Outside the door, though, he paused to hear any negative remarks Sid might add. There were several.

"Now another Warden's got us on their charity list! What's the matter with you? You and Lizzy are as tied to them as I am. Nobody can see it but me. I hate that family, and if I can find a way to get back at them for this, I will. Believe you me, I will."

seven

The heavy onslaught came in Beth's presence at home. She thought her father must have delayed the subject deliberately so he could use it to harass her.

Sid's face had not been its normal color since he approached the door of the kitchen. "Was this your idea?" he shrieked.

"What are you talking about, Pa?" she said, wiping her hands together over the breadboard to rid them of biscuit dough.

"You know what I'm talkin' about! Travis Warden comin' to the mills today to offer Fred a job at Riley Nugent's furniture business."

Beth threw her arms around Fred, and the hug was returned. "Oh, Fred! That's wonderful! When are you going to work for him?"

"Tomorrow morning." Beth tried to ignore Sid's smirk at the smile on her brother's face as Fred continued, "Mr. Travis says Mr. Nugent is going to train me to make furniture like he does." Breathlessly, he finished telling her the details.

Sid laughed his loudest. "Pore old Fred. He don't know it's a trap. I know a secret he don't. Mr. Riley Nugent won't have a body who's not a Bible believer working for him. He'll put the pressure on Fred to be 'saved.' But he's in for a surprise. This boy won't give in, and Nugent may decide he don't want him after all!"

Beth grabbed a dishcloth and finished wiping her hands. "That's not true, Fred. Travis wouldn't have brought the message if Mr. Nugent hadn't sent him. Riley Nugent won't go back on his word. Now you and Pa wash up for supper.

The biscuits are going in the oven, and we'll eat as soon as they're done."

Whether she had bluffed him out or her father was simply hungry, he let it go. Beth didn't care. She had every reason to dance a jig, and it took all her control to suppress the urge.

&

After supper at home, Travis read his Bible and spent time in prayer about the situation with Fred. Though he had talked to the boy in his father's presence, Sid had been angry. He wondered how his anger had affected Beth at home. Despite Sid's opinion, had Beth been happy about Fred's job? He'd like to know, but this was not the time to *accidentally* ride by the Faraday house in hopes of catching her coming from work. He'd find out later what he wanted to know. As a last resort, he'd visit Virgie.

His classes would start at the University of Pennsylvania in a few weeks. But he was still undecided whether to leave. He couldn't seem to get away from the fact that his father needed him for support. Warden Mills had extended the business to a new sawmill, and it was paying off in trade. His father could use his help in the near future. And he wanted to know Beth better. She might not be the girl God had for him, but if he stayed a little longer and prayed a little more, God might show him the answer.

He changed to more comfortable clothes and looked for a book he had mentioned to Virgie as one Beth might like to read. She absorbed literature like a sponge to water, and Travis had found out she read while walking back and forth to work. What a misuse of time, when she should be cuddled up on a lounge with a pillow to her back, enjoying a restful hour.

He felt his face warm. In his opinion, people with red hair blushed at inappropriate times. When his mind strayed to thoughts of Beth Faraday, his face always seemed to warm. It never happened with anyone else. He wasn't bashful.

Regardless of the other person's importance, talking religion or business or sports usually gave him no problem. Only thoughts of Beth had the power to disorient him. The warmth didn't lessen, and he grinned. Seeing her more might be the answer.

A light knock at the door made him wish he hadn't thought of her. His father stuck his head around the door and motioned him forward.

Mortimer wasn't concerned about Travis's face. His own face was flushed, and he was perspiring. "I need you," he whispered. "Come with me, please."

His father's command had the earmark of an emergency he was physically unable to handle. Travis quickly followed Mortimer out of the room. Making sure none of the help saw them leave the house, they arrived at an old shed, the hiding place, in seconds. Lit by a single piece of charcoal, the darkened room was empty.

"What's happening, Father?"

Mortimer surveyed the room and looked out a peephole in the wall. "There's a delay. Help may be needed. Can you follow the path to the river? Don't make any noise, and stay hidden until you see the men come up to the old rotted oak. Go to them quickly in case our guest is hurt. The conductor will leave as soon as he hands the visitor over to you. Now go!"

Wondering how many times this had happened, Travis slid through the door and took off down the path to the river. Halfway there, he met a man almost dragging someone smaller. Without a word, Travis and the conductor transferred the slave, and Travis grasped the smaller man securely in his arms. The husky boatman turned back to the river as Travis made for the shed.

The slave was not heavy. Travis had no problem carrying him. He didn't seem mortally wounded, but he couldn't walk. Travis hefted him up to get a better grip. The shed was just ahead.

His father opened the shed door and helped him get the wounded man to the pallet at the side of the room. With a knife, Travis sliced the man's pant leg to reveal a long, bleeding cut on his calf. It needed a thorough cleansing. His father opened a box under a small table near the bed. In the box Travis saw clean strips of muslin and two bottles of liquid. His father poured water from a pitcher into a bowl on the table and handed it to his son. Travis dampened cotton strips and gently washed the jagged cut.

As he worked, he realized the slave was a man about his own age. Though in pain, the black man hardly winced. No one talked. No one asked questions. The Underground Railroad was built on trust. The man who had brought the slave had disappeared without a word because he'd already done his part and knew Travis would do his.

The cut was as clean as Travis could make it, and he gave his father a questioning look. Mortimer picked up a covered object, and Travis grinned when he disclosed a jug of alcohol Sid Faraday would have liked to lay his hands on. He removed the plug and, with a quick grip on the slave's arm, signaled him to be quiet. The man nodded, and Travis splashed the cut with alcohol. The black man almost fainted, but he didn't make a sound.

Mortimer lowered his head, praying, and so did Travis. They opened their eyes as the injured man mouthed *thank you.*

Applying an abundant layer of healing ointment over the cut, Travis wrapped the wound in soft strips of linen and tied them in place with netting. Mortimer furnished a clean pair of work pants and helped the man put them on.

But he could not stand. Travis couldn't let him go. With a look, he conveyed the message that the man must spend the night. His father, unwrapping a plate of food for their guest, nodded agreement. When the patient was lying on the pallet again, they moved to leave, and Mortimer motioned to the slave to sleep. The man nodded.

A quarter moon had come out, and Mortimer signaled Travis to go on. Without a sound, Travis slipped out the door. Instead of going directly to the back door of the house, he headed for the barn. Suddenly, from the corner of his eye, he saw the shadow of a man flit by and lose itself in the trees at the corner of the smokehouse.

Someone had been watching! Travis whirled and ran toward the figure, but the man left the thicket and zipped away in the direction opposite to the river. Travis ran back to the shed. He knew without doubt the identity of the culprit.

❧

Sitting in Travis's darkened room later, they decided there was only one thing to do.

"Sid has been defiant all day long," said Mortimer. "It was as if he wanted to see how far he could go. I was thinking of replacing him, but that might be just what he wants. Now that Fred will be learning a new trade, he might see a future where Elizabeth and Fred support him while he sleeps in that old chair on his front porch."

Travis stretched out his long frame and crossed his arms. "Well, you can't do that now, in any case. We have to talk to him and appeal to his conscience, or better nature, or whatever we can grab onto. He's got us in a bind."

Snorting, his father frowned. "I have a lot of friends who want to put Sid Faraday in his place. If it came to the law, I think they'd stand up for me." He breathed a resigned sigh. "But people are people. Knowing the reprobate I was before I accepted Jesus, they might not risk their reputations and the well-being of their families to help. I might even have to do a few favors."

"No, Father! We can't have that." Travis rose and walked to the window. He paused, looked out, and then faced the older man. "We have to go to him, Papa. We have to talk to him right now, together, while it's fresh. Maybe he hasn't been drinking."

Mortimer rose. "Wait, Son. This is a dangerous decision. If it were just me, that's what I'd do. But now I've brought you into it. You're as guilty as I am, and you'll be treated the same. We have to think of what else can be done."

"There is nothing else. Let's go now. I came into this with my eyes wide open. Don't blame yourself." Travis paused. "Maybe Beth will help us. She might have a little influence on her father." But his voice was not optimistic.

"You call Elizabeth Beth now?" His father cocked an eyebrow. "Hmm."

Travis managed a smile. "Come on."

❧

Beth had gone to sleep early, but she was awakened by the knock at the door; and in her bedroom, she grabbed her wrapper from the closet. The walls were thin. She could hear every word. It was Travis and his father! What could be wrong? Was it about Fred's job?

She prayed, *Oh, Jesus, don't let this be trouble for Fred. He's so happy, and I'm so proud of him and grateful to the Nugents for this chance. Let this be something that can be smoothed over. Please, God.* She stood at the door and listened.

"What do ya want?" said her father brusquely.

Travis spoke first, and Beth's heart beat faster. "We want to talk to you about tonight."

"Come to bribe me, eh?" Sid's harsh laughter rang out.

"Why? Why should we want to bribe you?"

What had happened to make Mr. Warden and Travis come to the house? The fast beating of Beth's heart now reflected fear.

"Because I saw you breakin' the law by taking that black man in. You can't deny it. I saw you!"

Beth gasped. Could it be? Her black friend, Clara Watts,

had told her there were people who helped slaves get away to the North. The hard lives slaves endured under abusive owners forced them to that desperate decision. Clara's family was free, but they worried about a cousin, Tar, who was terribly mistreated in Alabama. Travis and Mr. Warden must have been trying to help someone, and her pa had caught them. She clasped her hands at her breast in frustration. If only she could do something!

"How do you know it wasn't a friend? Many people come to my parents' house. They have many friends."

"No, no," Sid snarled. "You don't carry a friend in your arms up to your house. This friend couldn't walk good. What you've got is a little station on the Underground Railroad, and you're a conductor! I got that straight. I ain't dumb."

Tears brimming Beth's eyes spilled down her cheeks. *How could you do this, Pa? They need help. You went clear out to the Wardens' place so you could spy on them. What can you want from them?* Almost immediately the question was answered for her.

Mr. Warden was the speaker. "Faraday, you have no idea how many times I've come within minutes of letting you go at the mills. Time after time when you came in drunk, I was tempted; but you have three children. I couldn't bring myself to do it. I hope you remember."

"Yeah, and sometimes I didn't even feel like comin' in, but I did. Don't *you* forget that! But it's all comin' to a head now."

Travis spoke with a somber voice. "Mr. Faraday, please reconsider. These poor people need help. My father only tried to do what's right, as he did with you. He tried to help black people who have served their masters well and have been beaten in return. Have a little compassion, won't you? You wouldn't like to be treated like that, either."

Sid said to Travis. "Let's stop for a minute. Something just dawned on me. Your son don't know the whole story, does he? What you did to me?"

Beth heard not a word from Mortimer.

Her father snickered. "That stopped you, didn't it?"

"What are you getting at?"

"Don't push me, or I'll give sonny the full treatment."

"What is he talking about, Father?" said Travis as if he felt a further threat.

"Why don't you tell him, *Mr.* Warden?" Beth heard the familiar smirk in her father's voice.

"What is it, Father? Speak openly, please," said Travis.

Mortimer sounded dead tired, and he apparently seated himself. "I suppose there's no way to avoid it. Sid seems determined that you know the complete, ugly story."

"Whose fault is that? Not mine."

The strain in Travis's voice was clear. "Talk, Father. Whatever it is, it can't be worse than this cat-and-mouse game we're playing."

Beth heard a long, drawn-out sigh, and Mortimer spoke again. "It happened a long time ago, before Sid's wife, Flora, died. As you know, I was a fool in those days. Nothing mattered to me but money. Sid and Flora bought this little house from me. It had belonged to my brother, Phil, who passed away when you were a boy."

"I remember," said Travis.

"Flora used money her grandmother left her to pay part of the loan. When her heart failed, Sid couldn't pay any more because he missed a lot of work and had three little kids to take care of. I'm ashamed to say I foreclosed on him. Flora passed away that same year.

"When I came to the Lord, I gave the house to Sid. I never had a chance to beg Flora's forgiveness. Elizabeth is just like Flora, gentle and sweet. But Sid started drinking—"

"Which I'd have never started if you hadn't taken everything away from me!"

Beth heard nothing from Mortimer for a few seconds, and

then he began again in a subdued tone.

"If you'll keep the underground to yourself, I'll keep you on at the mills for as long as you live," Mortimer pleaded.

"Please." Travis sounded as if he would have fallen to his knees.

Her father chortled with glee. "Now who's got the upper hand? Not you!" Sid laughed loudly. "All right. We're gonna do a little deal here, and you're gonna do what I say. We'll let this go for a while. But just remember, I can point you out anytime I want to—you and your fine, handsome boy."

"Let me add a word, Mr. Faraday. I haven't known about this, and the risk my father is taking is too great. He's too fragile to carry on the operation. He is a kind man who wanted to help those less fortunate than himself, but he must stop. You've made that point clear, and I thank you."

Beth felt as if she were choking. She was so ashamed of her father. She went back to sit on the bed, to wait until she heard the sound of their buggy going down the road. Then she crept out of her room.

Her father was practically dancing in the middle of the floor. "I'll bet you heard every word of that. I've got those high-flyin' snoots right where I want 'em. They'll do whatever I say from now on."

"But why, Pa? Why did you threaten them? They're only trying to help black people like Clara Watts's cousin. His owner beats him just to see him beg for mercy." She dried a tear that traced down her cheek. "Not all slave owners treat their people badly, but some do, and those are the ones they're trying to help. Can't you forget what you saw? Please? You heard what Travis said about his father. They're quitting the underground. Mr. Warden's health won't permit it."

Her father hardly noticed. "Yes, sir!" he said, pounding a fist into his other palm. "I've got 'em right where I want 'em."

Beth went back to bed. The tears she had held back came

readily. There was nothing she could do. Her father had been looking for an excuse to hurt the Wardens. What he had told his family about the Wardens' cruelty was untrue. Mr. Warden was a true gentleman. Even Travis might be different than Sid had portrayed him. The thought so moved her, she cried until sleep intervened.

●

She could hardly look at the Wardens that Sunday morning at church. Especially Travis. Each time she looked in his direction, he was watching her. Or did he think the same of her? Whichever was true, Beth felt they spent more time watching each other than the preacher, and she tried to corral her meandering thoughts. After church, she lost the power of control.

"Good morning, Miss Faraday."

Travis approached, looking handsome in gray trousers and a black coat. Evidently he had not ridden his horse; he was not wearing riding boots. Beth felt her face warm; and for some reason, Travis not only noticed, he appeared to enjoy it. She didn't like that, and it made her just angry enough to give her some backbone.

"So it is. . .or was." She turned away in embarrassment.

"Oh, come on, Beth. Don't be angry with me. I was in hopes we could talk awhile," he said with a contrite look.

It was enough for Beth. She opened her mouth to agree when Riley and Mary passed by on the way to their buggy.

"Are you hungry, Beth? Mary has fried chicken all ready at home," said Riley.

Stepping forward, Mary asked, "I don't suppose we could interest *you* in my fried chicken, could we, Travis? With potato salad? And a nice variety of vegetables? Blackberry cobbler for dessert," she added in an enticing tone.

"Are you sure it's not too much trouble?" At the shake of Mary's head and her little grin, Travis kissed her cheek. "Let me tell the folks I'll be home later. Riley, got enough room for me on that seat?"

"Sure! We'll wait."

As soon as Travis left, Beth let out a long breath. She was terrified. "Mary! What shall I talk about? I don't know how to talk to him. I only know how to defend myself when we quarrel."

"Then it's high time you learned," said Mary, and she took Beth's arm and pulled her along toward their buggy. "I won't make you sit with him, though. . .this time."

She climbed into the conveyance and beckoned Beth to sit beside her. Beth reached for something to hang onto to help her inside and felt a hand under her other elbow. Travis gently steadied her ascent into the buggy. Again, her face warmed; but Travis was looking at Riley, who had taken up the reins. Once Beth was settled, he sprang up beside Riley, and the horses responded to Riley's "Walk on!"

It took the whole ride to the Nugent home for Beth to calm down enough to pray and to deal rationally with her feelings about Travis. The problem was being objective about a man she'd fought with all her life and who now seemed determined to do her good. She asked the Lord to guide her every word when they got to the house. Otherwise, her disobedient tongue might betray their new beginning.

❧

"That was a meal any man would relish, Mary," said Travis. "Thank you for letting me come to enjoy it with you. May I pay for my meal by helping set the dining room to rights?"

"No, almost everything was taken care of before I left this morning."

"I'll help her," said Beth. "As convenient as her kitchen is, it won't take long at all." Beth was always fascinated with the time-saving cabinets and shelves Riley had built to assist Mary in the preparation of their meals.

Mary took two plates out of Beth's hands and pointed to the door. "Take her out of here, Travis. She works hard all week. For once I'd like to see her do something for pleasure. You can take a walk over to the pond or go sit in the swing under the maple tree. That's *my* pleasure spot to relax."

With an irresistible smile, Travis held out his hand. "Shall we?"

Beth glided past the hand and out the door, too concerned with the blush she felt to answer.

eight

Beth paused in the shade of a swaying willow and looked out over the water. "It's like a little lake, isn't it? Imagine looking out your window every day, seeing the water, hearing birds sing, watching squirrels play. It must be like living in a paradise."

They came to a stile over a fence near the water. Travis spread his handkerchief on one of the steps and invited Beth to sit. "We've come a long way since our childhood arguments, haven't we, Beth?"

Beth couldn't resist. "Except when you splash mud on my skirt, and I have to spend hours cleaning and pressing it." At his frozen face, she giggled. "Your expression just then made it all worthwhile," she said, and she shook her finger at him. "But don't try it again!"

He grabbed her hand. "I won't. I promise."

She stared at his hand. It was a big hand, a strong hand, the fingers long and slender. He let go, and she felt deprived of warmth.

Beth cleared her throat. "You said one day when we met that you were leaving. Did you go away?"

He snickered. "You're getting in your licks, Beth. You mean you didn't even know I was gone? I went to Philadelphia for a week."

"No, I didn't." She saw his doubt. "It's true. How would I have known? We weren't exactly friends."

He turned toward the pond. "I visited my sister and her husband. They want me to live with them and enroll at the University of Pennsylvania." His glance at her was hopeful.

Instead, Beth's eyes opened wide, and she gasped, "How can you say it so casually? I've never heard anything so wonderful. To go to school at a great university," she said in awe. "Travis, do you realize how blessed you are?"

"Yes, I do," he said seriously. "I need encouragement right now, so your enthusiasm is welcome. You're the first one I've talked to."

Beth stood to walk again, and he took her arm to support her on the unlevel path.

Travis spoke softly. "I've been praying the Lord will show me what He wants me to do with my life. At the Christian school I attended in Baltimore, I was praying about going into the ministry. I'd been waiting for an answer, but God hadn't given me a yes."

"You prayed about it. That's the important thing. I have to learn to pray like that. I want to do what Jesus tells me, but I'm not clear on the proper way to go about it. I've never been to school and never had a chance to read the Bible until now, with Mary and Virgie."

A sympathetic look swept his face. "Would you like to study the Bible with me, Beth?"

Looking up sharply, Beth saw that he really meant what he was saying. How could they possibly be together except for this one single day? Tears came to her eyes, and she looked away.

In the excitement of being with him, she had almost forgotten what had happened when he and his father came to the house that night. She didn't want to stumble into that subject. She didn't want him to know she had heard everything they said. Though it was to her family's shame, for the Wardens there was real danger. It was best to keep it to herself.

"So, Philadelphia. How did it turn out?" she said quickly.

"I got my answer." He stopped, and dropping his hand

from her arm, he propped his foot on a natural stone seat the Nugents had hauled to the pond. "It seems now as if the answer has been there all along. I had to wait for God's time. I met a group of medical students at the university and got to view a few classes. It was the most interesting thing I've ever done, Beth. God fulfilled His promise to me. It was like He was saying, 'This, too, is My work.' What a moment! It was fine!"

His expression told her he couldn't begin to describe it. She wanted to clap or shout with happiness. What must it feel like to examine feelings like that? He was living that spectacular moment over again, and she was there with him to enjoy it.

"Tell me more," she begged.

He smiled at her, and they sat together on the stone seat. "I spent the whole day learning what it was like to study medicine. It was as if I knew, every hour, what was coming next, and I was ready for it. Can you understand?"

"I've never had an experience like that, but I'd like to. You should treasure it."

"I do, *and* what happened after that." He leaned closer as he spoke. "I went to a chapel to find a quiet place alone, and I spent time in prayer. Clearly, as if it had been arranged from the beginning, I knew God wanted me to study medicine."

"Not be a preacher."

He shook his head. "Not be a preacher."

"Well, I can see why. A doctor who believes in Jesus Christ can minister for the Lord with every patient he treats," she said solemnly, wondering why she was being allowed to listen to Travis. He said she was the first person he had told. . .the very first person.

"You're right. I'm convinced He thinks I can be more useful to Him as a doctor than as a minister. There are many things going on right now to discourage me; but God wants me to be faithful, no matter what, and I will be."

Beth remembered the day they talked at her house, and she had wondered if he was a true Christian. If only she'd tried harder to know him. She wished she could talk with him about her father's ominous wish to get even with the Warden family. She wished that, together, they could turn the frightful situation around. They both knew about it. Still, she couldn't bring herself to open the subject.

"Follow the path you feel God wants you to pursue, Travis. I hope it all goes the way you want it to and that you'll live happily with your family in Philadelphia."

"I may not go until after Christmas. There are. . .uh, circumstances that might prevent my leaving before then." He stood and held out his hand to help her to her feet. "Now since you know the future plans I believe God has for me, what about you? What are you praying for?"

Beth hoped her face didn't betray the shock she felt. If he knew how often she had prayed for him and for his father, he'd be amazed.

❧

Travis tried to keep his face without expression. She knew. He could see it in her face. What a time for it to happen.

It had been a perfect day. When he woke up this morning, he had been looking forward to the worship service only. But since then, there had been a delightful lunch with the Nugents and Beth, and he was spending an unbelievable hour with her. She had encouraged him in his plans for the future. Beth! The tyrant who gave him nightmares as a kid!

Lizzy was grown now, and with the charming, intriguing Beth had come a problem far larger than a mere disagreement. She was the daughter of the man who could report his father and him to the authorities for harboring a runaway slave. Sid Faraday knew it all, and he could turn on them at the least provocation.

He wondered why God had brought this developing

friendship about. Was it to delay his move to Philadelphia so he could be part of the passage of events at his family home? A delay seemed realistic. He'd be there if there was a problem, and he was determined to talk his father out of keeping the station. He'd never seen his father so distressed as when pleading with Sid Faraday, a man nowhere near Mortimer's stature.

Also, if he delayed his move, he and Beth could become closer. Did he want that? He did. He longed to see Beth rise to a better position among her peers and to develop as a lady, unhindered by her father's sad reputation. In the next few months, if he stayed, he could see that happening. The smile he felt emerged. The decision was made. He'd stay. And that was that.

Now they had to settle the other thing.

"So should we get our big problem out in the open and talk about it?" he said as they ambled on.

"With innuendos and knowing looks passing back and forth, I suppose it's silly to avoid it." She looked up at the cloudy sky that had blown in while they were outside and murmured, "Looks like the weather has changed with our mood."

She crossed her arms at her chest. "I overheard your conversation the other night when you and your father came by. I've wanted to tell you how sorry I am. My father is without principle. I try to respect him, but when I know he does these terrible things, it's hard. What can I say? Apologies mean nothing." Beth covered her mouth to hold back a sob.

Travis placed his hand on her shoulder. "Let's go and sit in the swing." He watched her retrieve a small handkerchief from her pocket to wipe her eyes. "I know there's a problem with your father that you can't solve. That's the first thing I want to address. My family doesn't blame you or your brothers for any of it. Next, we Wardens can't solve the problem, either. Don't you agree?"

She nodded, and Travis continued, "Get ready now. I'm going to be Virgie the Teacher. Smile!" And she did. In a patient voice, he said, "What do we do when we have a problem we can't solve? We go to God. We pray. Psalm 40:13 says, 'Be pleased, O Lord, to deliver me: O Lord, make haste to help me.' Even David the king begged, seeking God's help, just as we must. God has the answer for our dilemma, Beth. *Believe* that He will work it out."

Her answer was sincere. "I'll try. I really will try."

"I know you will." He gave the swing a push with his foot, and it creaked into motion. "Now that we've shared our anxiety about this crisis, I hope you'll let me know if there is any way we can avoid conflict with Sid."

Beth leaned back in the swing. "I don't think it's possible, Travis. I never know what he's thinking." She sat up straight again. "I didn't say thank you for getting Fred's job for him. How did you manage it?"

"I didn't. I just delivered the message. Riley thought if I took it, there would be no question as to how the Wardens felt about Fred's leaving the mills. I did run into your father, however. Afterward, I paused outside the door to hear a few choice words he offered in my behalf."

She reached out and touched his arm. "I'm sorry, Travis. I heard a few of those when he got home."

He captured her hand. "We're friends from now on, Beth. I'll try not to hurt your feelings like I did that day years ago when I told you to learn to be a lady. You've become very much the lady now."

"Mary and Virgie have helped me so much. They've been very good to me. And, yes, I'd like to be friends instead of enemies."

"Will you pray with me that this war between our fathers will be resolved?"

"Of course. You pray, and I'll listen."

Her open expression removed any doubt. Beth Faraday was definitely God-given wife material.

28

The buggy bounced along to the crossroads, then turned toward the mound on which the Warden house sat.

"Virgie, I'm so nervous," wailed Beth. "What if my father hears of this? I couldn't possibly supply a good enough explanation."

Virgie slapped the reins of the horse and urged him to go faster. "Don't fret. We won't stay long. I want you to see the quilt Mother has in the frame. A lady should know how to quilt with neat, invisible stitches; and today you will see the best example I can show you."

"I appreciate the fact you're teaching me something new, but—"

"Never you mind, Beth. We're almost there. See? There's Mother waving from the dining room window."

Distracted by the large stone mansion ahead, Beth had a hard time finding the right window. Then she saw her. Small and pretty, Gwendolyn Warden was an impressive lady. Beth had seen her several times in the settlement before the Wardens had spoken to her at church; yet since her father's upsetting "deal" with the Wardens, she had not been eager to cross paths with any of the Wardens except Travis.

The horse and buggy taken care of by a servant, Virgie walked briskly into the house, Beth following. The beautiful furnishings that confronted her inside slowed her forward momentum. To say the house was more splendid than Virgie's was an understatement. She had heard how beautiful it was, but she was unprepared for the fine selection of rich woods, shining floors, and thick carpets. Marvelous paintings and portraits lined the walls. The beauty she beheld was dreamlike. She felt the Lord had blessed her with eyesight to see this house.

"Hurry along, Beth. You're the one who's dallying now," taunted Virgie.

Beth followed quickly, and Mrs. Warden, looking exceptionally lovely in a dark green day dress, met them near the staircase. As always, her gray hair was neatly bound in an attractive bun at the back of her head. Beth dipped a small curtsey.

"Now none of that. We're friends. Virgie has been telling me how neat your needlework is, and I thought you might like to see the process of quilting. Let's go along." She started toward the back of the house.

"Thank you, Mrs. Warden. This is very nice of you."

Mother and daughter spoke briefly about family matters, and then Gwendolyn opened the door to a light, plastered room with shelves holding bolts of fabric and spools of cotton. On a table at one side, a muslin pattern was laid out. Cabinets lined another wall, and Beth could only imagine the quantity of sewing supplies within.

A large frame containing a quilt, rolled from both ends, hung by ropes from hooks attached to the ceiling. Two chairs were drawn up to the far side of the quilt, and another chair sat next to the windows.

Beth could hardly speak. She had seen comforters and quilts, many created with special care to be as beautiful as the owner could make them. But this! It was like a flower garden blooming inside the house. The colors were bright and varied, and they set up the illusion of dimension within the flat surface. It was glorious. With all her heart, she wished she could one day create such a beautiful bedcovering.

"Would you like to learn, Beth?" asked Gwendolyn.

"Yes. Oh, yes. How do you start?"

For the next hour, Gwendolyn taught her how to begin. First, muslin was the quilt's backing. Layered on it was cotton or wool to give the quilt warmth. Stretched over the padding was the delightful covering of hundreds of quilt pieces that had taken untold hours to assemble. The edges were bound last.

"The first thing you need to learn is that quilting is a labor of love, Beth," said Gwendolyn. "I think of it as pleasurable work that wraps my family with my love. All my children have quilts I have made for them."

In her mind Beth saw the children's homes as Mrs. Warden had described. What would it be like to belong to such a family?

She spent only a short time with Mrs. Warden, but that time was priceless. They chatted while the older lady worked on the quilt with what Virgie had termed "invisible stitches." Beth liked Travis's mother, and she felt it was returned. Virgie's friendship, too, rose to a new level. To Beth, the day was perfect in every way—up to a point.

Chuckling, Virgie and Gwendolyn remembered altercations between Travis and Beth as children, and they told them with ease and exaggeration. Beth's face flushed with embarrassment until she finally relaxed and added recollections of her own that were new to the other two. So many giggles and so much laughter with Travis's family made a perfect day even better, and Beth was sad when it ended.

Virgie ordered the buggy, and soon they were headed for the village. At the crossroads they met Travis riding home on Hero. Virgie slapped the reins and speeded up to discourage him from following them. But he didn't try.

"I didn't think we should take time for another visit, but he obviously didn't realize it was us," she said thoughtfully. "I wonder why he had such a frown on his face?"

A quarter of a mile farther, Beth saw a familiar figure going their way. It was her friend, Clara Watts. Virgie saw her, too.

"Let's stop. I need to ask her a favor." Virgie pulled to a

stop. "Can we take you to town, Clara?" she called.

Clara's eyes widened. "I'd be obliged," she answered, climbing in beside Beth. "How come you're with Miz Bower, Lizzy?" she said softly as Virgie urged the horse to continue.

"We're good friends, Clara," said Virgie. "Beth's helping me with a few household tasks each week. That's why I stopped. Would you be able to help us one day, say, Monday? I'd like to put up some curtains Beth and I have been working on. I get dizzy when I try to climb up high, and the day would give you two girls a chance to be together."

At Clara's look of surprise, Beth nodded. "Do come, Clara. I'd like to be with you again. I've missed you." Beth put her arm around her friend and smiled.

"Me, too," said Clara. "But your old man's too mean for me. So's your brother, Charlie. He don't like me, and I don't like him."

"I'm sorry, Clara." Beth took her arm down. "I wish I could make it up to you for the way they've treated you, but I can't. Tell me, have you had any word about your cousin, Tar?"

"Not since my aunt wrote our preacher last month. She asked us all to be praying about Tar. He let a rabbit out of one of his owner's traps. They'd forgot the trap, and the rabbit was starving. The foreman saw Tar with the rabbit in his hand, and he accused him of stealin' it. Tar got a terrible beating."

"Clara, I'm so sorry."

Is that all I can say? Just "I'm sorry"? Poor Tar. Poor Clara and her family. No wonder Mr. Warden tries to help the runaways. Who wouldn't? Pa wouldn't. And he wants to hurt anyone who tries.

Dear Lord, help us all. The Watts, the Wardens, and us, dear Lord. Help our family do a turnaround to let You guide our lives. My father and brothers need You, and I need You in my life every day. Be with me, please, Lord.

Although she felt like crying, she dared not let her tears go. Had Travis heard Clara's tale of tragedy before they met him on the road? Of course. His inattention to them told of the turmoil in his heart. It was her turmoil, too. No one in the buggy knew the facts as she and Travis did. Was there nothing they could do? Nothing *she* could do?

nine

The Harvest Festival at church granted Beth a chance to be with Travis again. Despite condemnation from Sid for the few hours she spent at it, Beth happily helped decorate a church booth with autumn leaves, pumpkins, and cornstalks.

She had a new brown dress for the festival, courtesy of Mary and Virgie. Rows of ecru tatting at the yoke and three tiers around the sleeves softened the look of the dark material. That handcraft skill was Beth's now. Virgie taught her to create the delicate lace to trim clothing and added the hint that she could use tatting on linens "in her future home." Beth was not as optimistic as Virgie. She wondered if such a thing as her future home would ever exist.

It was difficult to keep knowledge of her friendship with Travis from her father. Mary had helped by making her evening at the festival possible. Unannounced, she arrived at the house in her buggy, tied up the horse, and marched up to the door. Beth had been watching for her.

"I've come for Elizabeth, Mr. Faraday," she said as soon as she was inside. "I'm sure her work is done for the day, and the family has eaten; so I'd like to take her for an evening with her friends at church. You, Fred, and Charlie are welcome to come along, if you will. I have my buggy right outside."

"Make her take Fred, Pa. Not me," Charlie declared scornfully.

Beth, standing back to let Mary work her knowing wiles on Sid, said nothing. But Mary saw it a different way.

"An excellent idea. Fred, come with us. I know you'll have a fine time, and you'll meet many nice people. I'll bring you both home."

Fred smiled his pleasure, but Sid was infuriated.

"Go ahead and take him. He spends most of his time with your husband, anyway," he said, referring to Fred's job with Riley's furniture business.

"Oh, I'm glad you reminded me, Mr. Faraday. Riley wanted me to tell you what a fine job Fred is doing at work. He learns quickly and is very dependable. Of course, you taught him to be prompt for work, didn't you?"

"You bet I did. That's one of my best marks."

"I'm sure." Mary took her handbag from the sofa where she had set it. "Well, Elizabeth and Fred, let's be on our way."

The three left quickly, and Beth breathed a sigh of relief.

❧

At Mary's house, Beth changed into her new brown dress. When they arrived at the torch-lit fair, Riley took Fred away to show him some wood samples that were on display by the Warden sawmill.

As the ladies approached the booth Beth had helped decorate, Mary called out to two sisters in charge of the display. "Hello, Nema! Hello, Nell! All ready for a big crowd?" Both ladies responded in excited voices.

"Nema, do you want Mary and me to take your places for a while?" Beth asked the taller lady. "You could walk around and see the rest of the exhibits."

"We've only been here an hour, but I would like to get a look at the other booths. Wouldn't you, Nell?"

Her companion, a heavyset lady, clapped her tiny hands. "Oh, yes! It's all so thrilling."

They strolled away, and Mary and Beth familiarized themselves with prices of the handmade articles and pies that the ladies of the church had created for the benefit of the benevolent fund. The variety of the display was exceptional.

"I'll take a slab of apple pie, ma'am."

Beth glanced up. Travis, dressed in a tan coat and black

riding breeches and boots, was startlingly handsome. When he took off his hat, his crisp red hair glistened in the torchlight, and the scent of his shaving lotion enchanted her. Her heart rejected a normal beat. *By any measure, Travis Warden, you are outstanding. But you'll never hear it from me.*

"I'm sorry, sir. We sell only whole pies. We aren't equipped to sell 'slabs.'"

"Oh, I think we could make an exception, Beth. Riley and Fred will probably come begging before the night is over," said Mary impishly.

Beth felt like teasing, too. "I suppose so, and I wouldn't want my brother to go hungry. Do you have a pocketknife, Mr. Warden? I can find a napkin to help you hold the pie," Beth said more seriously.

"I do appreciate it, Miss Faraday," he said. "Would you care for a walk when I finish my dessert?"

"And don't say you have to stay here," Mary exclaimed, handing Beth a napkin. "You decorated; I didn't. I'll watch the booth. Besides, Nema and Nell will be back before the real crowd gets here."

Unable to resist, Beth gathered up her coat and handbag while Travis paid. When he finished his pie, he helped Beth with her wrap, and they set off.

"I talked to Fred. I'm glad you were able to get him out of the house. Riley said he's been working hard and deserves a good time. When I saw him last, he was with a bunch of his friends at the darts booth."

Around the church property, more members, including a fiddler and a banjo player who entertained, were showing up to enjoy the displays and booths of the festival. The couple wandered the complete circuit of what the fair offered and eventually stopped in front of the church to sit on the steps of the entryway.

"I'm glad you could come tonight, Beth. Mary told me she

was going by your house to get you. Did Sid give her any trouble?"

"I think it's hard for Pa to turn her down. He's a little afraid of her. Your sister, too."

"But he's not afraid of you. Though we're standing in the midst of a crowd of people, he'd believe the worst if he knew you and I were talking," he said grimly. "I'm afraid for you, Beth."

"No more than I am for you," she said, her voice breaking. "I have to ask you a question, Travis. Have you talked lately to Clara Watts?"

"Well, I might have spoken to her at one time or another. Why do you ask?" he replied, clearly stalling.

Beth creased a fold in the skirt of her dress. "The last time I saw her I. . .I got the idea that she had mentioned her cousin Tar to you. Clara and I talked after I went with Virgie to visit your mother, and Clara described Tar's latest abuse by his owner."

Travis stood to allow two ladies to enter the church, then he sat beside Beth again. "I haven't told my father about Clara's request," he said softly. "He'll want to get the man out of there."

"No, Travis! You can't!"

"Can't what?" It was Fred.

Travis jumped to his feet again, and Beth waited to hear what he would say.

"Your sister thinks I can't jump Hero over that board fence beside the church. I say I can. I guess I'll just have to come here someday and prove it to her," he said, grinning at Beth.

Fred instantly fell in with the myth. "He probably can, Beth," he said. "Hero's a good jumper."

"I guess I'll take his word for it then," she said and laughed nervously.

"Mr. Travis, I guess that's the first time she ever took your word for anything. When she was younger, she would have biffed you in the nose."

Despite the joke, Beth knew they had come close to disaster. Neither wanted Fred to know anything about the underground. But she needed to talk to Travis. Though he had deftly avoided the issue of Clara, she could tell he was thinking about it. Once, he'd said he intended persuading his father to close down the station. Was it still true?

"Beth and I have called a truce, Fred. You can do that when you're both Christians. What do you think about Beth coming to the Lord? My family and I think she made an excellent decision."

Fred looked around, then grinned slightly. "I don't feel mad like Pa does. I don't mind if other people get saved. I might do it someday. I know I've done wrong things. But it has to happen someplace besides church. I don't go to church."

"Sit here with Beth," said Travis. He backed up a few steps to let the boy sit down, and continued. "People don't have to be in church to let Jesus into their hearts, Fred. It can happen right where you are. He wants to forgive your sins and be your best friend. All you have to do is say, 'Jesus, please come into my heart. I give You my life.' In that moment, He will come to live in you, and you will never be alone or without Him again."

Fred held up his hand to stop him. "I can't say that yet. Pa will hate me if I do."

"Does he hate Beth?" Travis asked unsteadily.

With a sober face, Fred answered, "I don't know what he thinks anymore. He just lives out the days. When Ma died, I think he put an end to *feeling*. The word *hate* means as much to him as the word *love*."

"I'm sorry for your father. There's more to life than simply living out our days. That's why Jesus came, to give us a better life than just an ordinary one." Travis clasped Fred's shoulder.

"If you ever want to talk about the Savior I trust, I wish you'd come to see me, Fred. Maybe we can answer some questions that are bothering you."

"Yes, sir. Thank you." Fred turned and walked away.

❧

The next morning Travis rode to meet Beth as she walked toward Virgie's. She had time to assemble a full blush by the time their eyes met. She knew her face was flushed; she felt the warmth.

"I thought I might run into you if I came this way," he said, bending down to make eye contact. "Let me take you to the house."

"Travis, stop it!" Beth stepped away from him and brushed her apron smooth. "I can't get up there where everybody can see. What if someone comes by?"

"They'd see a pretty girl in her work clothes. She has soft blond hair with a braid tumbling down her back. Her eyes are blue, she has a pert little nose, and, altogether, her face is quite lovely."

He'd mesmerized her with his soft words and gentle look. When she broke the spell, she tried to explain. "Be reasonable. If I rode up to Virgie's with you, even she might tell your father, to say nothing of the servants. And what do you think he'd say about our being together at the festival? How could he trust me? I'm the daughter of his enemy."

"My mother likes you, and from what I've seen, so does my father. He realizes children are not responsible for what their parents do." He shook his head as if to clear his mind. "You're not responsible for what I do, either."

"Yes, I am, if the way I act puts you in jeopardy. I want to protect you—"

"But you don't have to."

"Yes, I do!"

Travis leaned down. Closing the distance between them,

he took her chin in his palm and kissed her gently. His gaze stayed on her as he pulled away.

"Travis. . ."

Finally, Beth's nerves alerted her to look back at the road. No one was around, but she couldn't let the intimacy continue. She ran. Once more she left him, with a puzzled look, in the middle of the road.

&

Had he really kissed Beth? After all the years of simply tolerating her, had all those violent emotions turned to love? It was odd, yet Travis couldn't keep from smiling.

Her tiny figure, as she ran, enthralled him. Beth was always a strong girl, healthy, energetic. She had proven it by besting him at outdoor games more than once. But mostly they had battled it out with every word weapon at their command. Now he could think of nothing more satisfying than being in her company. And it had evolved out of the most unlikely of reasons.

A frown replaced his smile, for he had no answers to the predicament that faced them now. Beth had no influence on her father. He had hoped that in time she could persuade Sid to let up on the Wardens. But that was a vain wish. Now Travis's desire was to get her away from Sid.

Wait a minute, Lord. I don't think You put that thought in my mind. Not after giving me this obsession to study medicine. I'd be in Philadelphia now if I hadn't wanted to support my father and help him get the sawmill in operation. Travis bowed his head, this time in shame.

Forgive me, Father, for threatening You with my own will. The truth is, I felt it imperative to know Beth better. No, I have to be honest, Lord. She was the main reason I stayed here. Contrite, he finished his prayer.

But his father *did* need him. They had both stood watch against Sid Faraday's movements and tried to ferret out his intentions. There had been no transfer in the Underground Railroad for a time, and then Clara Watts had approached him as he rode Hero home that day.

Clara was an intelligent young girl, one he trusted. When she stopped him and asked to speak to him, he gladly complied. Her story struck his heart like a swift arrow. He wanted to help get her cousin away from his maniacal owner.

But it would mean putting his father in the very position from which Travis wanted him extracted. All he had to do was ask Mortimer to help, and it would be done. But at what cost? It could surely be arranged. He could help it happen; although the consequences could cut him off from Beth forever.

He brought Hero to a canter and tried to remember their kiss. But the arrow in his heart was pitiless. All he felt was its pain.

❧

He had kissed her! Right there, on the road, leaning down to her, he had kissed her. Travis Warden!

Beth's feet could not fly fast enough. Virgie's front gate was straight ahead, but she was not near ready to go inside and be seen. Her burning face could ignite kindling. She looked at her hands. They were trembling. Her whole body was shaking. She hid herself in the shadow of the porch roof.

How different she felt than when they were young. They had disliked each other. Nothing had given her greater joy than making him look ridiculous. It was a stupid thing to want, and she regretted it. Looking back on their feud now, she admitted to a warped perspective. While he was growing in Christ, she was stifled by hate and prejudice. She had cheated her character of its ability to grow as Jesus meant her to.

Travis looked so handsome. In tan riding breeches, his dark blue coat making his white shirt look even whiter, brown boots, and a tall hat, his appearance was flawless. He could have any girl he wanted, and he had kissed *her*.

Society had set hard rules for a girl as poor as she. He was the son of the wealthiest family for miles around, a doctor in the making. She was a complete nobody. They weren't supposed to be attracted to one another. But she had Jesus Christ. Everything she had learned from her pastor, Mary, Virgie, and Travis confirmed that fact as a leveler of people. In God's eyes, she and Travis were equals.

Soon he'd leave for Philadelphia. She wouldn't meet him on the road to Virgie's or anywhere else. There would be girls who were smarter and more sophisticated in the city, and as it was here, he could have his pick. A great cloud of loneliness took her by surprise.

But there was a further obstacle, and it was worst of all: her father's threat to bring down the law on Mr. Warden and Travis if they dared help another slave. At this moment she knew Travis was mulling over in his mind the possibility of helping Clara's cousin escape his evil owner. The thought caused her to shiver.

Virgie slipped out the front door and squealed. "Oh! Beth! You scared me. What are you doing out here by yourself? Couldn't you get the door open?"

"I haven't tried. I. . .uh, was thinking about something."

"Yes, I think I see the problem." Virgie raised her hand to wave at the road, where Travis, with a crimson face, sat on Hero. Her brother returned her wave and rode quickly away.

Beth's face, even in shadow, was cast with a similar glow. Virgie giggled. "As you see, I got rid of that problem for you. Shall we go in?"

Head down, Beth passed through the door ahead of Virgie.

"I think we need to talk, Beth," her friend murmured.

Beth was frightened. Did Virgie suspect what her father and Travis were involved in? She prayed God would spare her from answering questions that might bring the truth to light. But she had to be truthful. She felt as trapped as she had when the Warden men came to beg Sid's cooperation and were refused.

Virgie opened the study door. "Let's go in here. The housekeeper's through with this room. We won't be disturbed." Virgie took a seat on the small sofa and motioned Beth to sit beside her.

"Are you and Travis seeing each other socially?"

It's just as I thought. She's unhappy about it. Their family has probably talked and decided she is the one to break it to me. They don't want Travis tangled up with a poor girl. That's why his face turned red when she saw him. Oh, please help me, Jesus. I only want the best for him.

Tears started in her eyes. "I—"

"I only want the best for him, Beth. And you *are* the best. I'm sorry I interrupted you, but I had to tell you that before you said anything else."

Beth felt tears shine a path down her cheeks, and she smiled, too. Virgie put her arms around her, and they cuddled close.

"I don't know exactly what I feel because it's so different than the way we started out. I don't know how he feels, either. He gave me a ride partway home the day you were expecting company from New York."

"I remember. You were so tired, dear." Virgie lovingly brushed a strand of Beth's hair back toward her braid.

"We talked at the Harvest Festival, too. Today we met on the road."

"He was here to pick up some business letters Conrad had for Papa. What happened?"

Scarlet best described the color of Beth's face.

Virgie giggled. "I'm sorry. I didn't realize I was being too personal."

They both laughed, but Beth was self-conscious. "Could we change the subject?"

"Yes. In fact, I had a special subject to bring up." Virgie checked the contents of a covered glass candy dish on a table to her left. "Beth, Mother and I are wondering if you'd like to join us in our new project. We sew garments for the needy. If you'd like to do this, it could be part of the tasks you do for me."

Beth wondered why Virgie's voice had turned so serious. "Why, yes, if you think I can be handy at it. I'd like to help."

"Good. Now we won't have one certain day for our sewing. We'll do our project when Mother decides it's needed." Virgie lowered her gaze. "There's one thing more. We'd rather you not tell anyone about this. Do you agree?"

In the back of Beth's mind rose an urge to find out the reason for the sewing project. Yet instinct told her she must not ask questions.

ten

Christmas was on the way. Beth and Travis saw each other from time to time during the week, but always on Sunday.

Travis made sure he kept out of Sid Faraday's way both at work and at home. Though Sid showed no soft feelings for his daughter, Travis feared any obvious friendship between the two would bring Sid's wrath down on Beth with a vengeance.

With Mary Nugent and his sister Virgie, however, he planned for future Christmas parties when Beth could be seen as a guest of one of those ladies, whose names Sid could *almost* speak aloud. In between times, Travis counted on the possibility of a few accidental meetings. And meet they did.

As time for his move to Philadelphia drew closer, Travis did not remind Beth by word or deed. He felt a long, drawn-out good-bye was cruel and unnecessary. He wanted her goodwill every day until he left. His love for her was growing. The details of God's plan were still beyond his knowledge, and he'd lost several hours of sleep praying for patience to wait for an answer.

After one of those sleepless nights, he came down to breakfast in the dining room, and his mother detected his lackluster spirit.

"Travis, you look as if you hadn't slept an hour. Are you ill?"

"No, but you're right about my not sleeping. I can't explain it."

"Are you worried about school?" His mother poured his tea from a silver service on the table at her right hand. "If you feel led, you can delay it further."

The girl set his breakfast before him, curtseyed, and

quickly left the room. He picked up his fork. "I feel it urgent to get into classes as soon as possible. Now that I have both your and Father's approval for changing my study program, I'm eager to proceed. I'm reading some of the recommended medical volumes, but after sitting in with instructors, I know I'm robbing myself by not studying at the university now."

"Why don't you go on? Much as I'd like it, you don't have to wait for Christmas at home."

Travis was letting his mother worry for no reason. "I still have personal affairs to settle before I go and some investments to rearrange," he said, a sad tone in his voice.

"You know your father said the same thing to me this morning before he left. He informed me he's drawing up a new will, of all things, in case something happens to him." Gwendolyn sipped from her cup and dabbed her lips with her napkin. "I hate talking about subjects like that. He thinks I don't know the real reason."

Travis's hand trembled, and he gripped his cup tighter. "Mother, what do you mean?"

Gwendolyn looked quickly toward the kitchen door, then leaned toward him. "I've known since the beginning."

Travis could do nothing but stare. His mother was as strong as his father had claimed she was. "This is a shock, Mother. Have you any other information your baby son should know?"

His mother's giggle was girlish. "Men. Their reactions are so predictable. As for other information, I'll tell you. Virgie and I have enlisted Beth Faraday in a pact you don't know about but should approve. She is a very good seamstress."

"Seamstress? Mother, are you hiring her to make clothing?"

Gwendolyn's face reflected the insult. "Certainly not!" She lowered her voice. "If you'll be calm, I'll explain. Beth can keep a secret. Can you?" At his nod, she continued. "Virgie and I have decided to become actively involved. Up to now, your father has acquired garments from any source available for the *friends* who visit us. Virgie and I have added to the supply as we were able, and now we have enlisted a third enthusiast in the sewing bee. Miss Beth Faraday."

Travis's feelings vacillated between happy and sad. Now Beth was into the underground as much as he. It showed her kindness and objectivity, but the danger was real. He wanted to protect her, not expose her to the same punishment that would befall the Wardens if they were caught.

"Mother, are you sure you realize how serious this thing is? It's a crime to help a slave escape from his owner. When we do this, we run afoul of the law. Are you and Virgie and Beth aware of that?"

"Of course we are. But all three of us are aware of a higher law. We believe Jesus means us to help His children who are abused and mistreated. His love is our example. In his letter to the Ephesians, the apostle Paul called Jesus the chief cornerstone 'in whom all the building fitly framed together groweth unto an holy temple in the Lord.' We are all part of the same building, Travis, and Jesus is the cornerstone."

"Beth is a new Christian. Do you think she grasps the significance of what she's doing?"

"She has been reaching out for the Lord for many years. Now that she has found Him, she is determined not to waste time. On top of that, she has a heart full of concern and understanding."

"I'd like to ask you a question, Mother. I value your opinion. As you believe Beth is developing in her relationship to Christ, do you believe God has a special place for her in His service?" Travis ventured.

"Indeed I do. And this is my further opinion. Elizabeth Faraday will be a wonderful wife and mother. From the first day of her salvation, she has had an outstanding servant heart. Mary Nugent loaned Beth a Bible that she studies, and her actions show she's living the Word as she absorbs it. I think some of us should arrange for a Bible of her own as a Christmas present."

"It's attended to already," he said, grinning. "Not that I want to change the subject, but have you heard when Carrie and Graham will get here?"

"They are looking at the Wednesday before Christmas. It depends on whether they can get a train the night before. Mortimer thinks the Philadelphia, Wilmington, and Baltimore has the right schedule. They'd like to be here ahead of the Nugent party on Friday night."

※

"So yer goin' to a party at your highborn church friends' instead of takin' care of your family, eh?" Sid's anger spilled over without warning.

Veins in her father's neck enlarged with his fury, and remembering how quickly her mother was taken, Beth momentarily wondered if she should stay home. As the oldest child, she felt it her duty to care for him. If he didn't calm down, she might lose her father, too. She had heard of a man—a strong, healthy farmer—who'd died when he got too angry.

Fred put his hand on Sid's shoulder. "Miz Nugent had me bring a special paper to invite Beth, Pa. If you'll let her go, I'll chop the wood you said you owed Abner Knoff as a favor."

Beth didn't like the sound of that. Her frown warned Fred, but he paid no attention. She knew why. He was determined that nothing would keep her from going to the Nugents' Christmas celebration.

"I was invited, too," he added. "But I said, 'No, I'd rather stay home with my pa that night.'" He did not look at Beth again.

His thoughtfulness warmed her heart. Fred knew the way their father's mind worked. She had a better chance of going if Fred stayed at home. *Oh, my sweet brother, what a treasure you are. Lord Jesus, take him into Your fold quickly, I beg You.*

Bitter words fell from Sid's mouth sharply and often, but Beth hardly heard. Defending herself was a waste of time. Thoughts of the evening ahead were far more pleasurable.

For the next hour, she would work fast to finish her tasks, and then she would bathe and put on the blue dress Virgie had made for her. She had everything laid out and ready. Then, to look taller, she intended to pile her hair up on her head in a ladylike fashion. Maybe Travis would notice.

Virgie and Conrad would be at the Nugents' tonight, as well as Virgie's brothers, Caleb and Joshua, and their families. Beth knew that group only by sight. What an exciting time it would be, getting to know more of the Wardens.

☙

The Nugents' buggy, driven by a servant, arrived at the appropriate moment to save Beth from further negative comments about her evening. Fred followed her out of the house and helped her climb into the buggy. It hurt Beth to see him so sad.

"You wish you were going, too, don't you, Fred?" she asked.

"I guess. Yeah. But you have a good time for me. I may go over to the Kinchloes' after a while. Pa will drink and then go off to sleep. Charlie's gone, too. Don't know where."

"I hope you have a good time at the neighbors'." Beth kissed his cheek. "Fred, someday we'll get out of this. God will give us families of our own. We'll treat them better than we've been. I think this is our training ground. We are learning. Both of us. You're learning a trade you can use anywhere, and you'll be able to support yourself. I'm learning to do many things, and I have the Lord. Accepting Jesus has made all the difference in my life. Pa can't really hurt me anymore. Do you understand?"

"Yes, I can see it for myself," Fred agreed.

"Will you think about this tonight? Anytime is the right

time to let Jesus into your heart."

Fred stood watching until the buggy turned the corner, and Beth could no longer see him. But a moment later, out of sight of the house, a different scene befell her.

"May I ride along with you, Miss Faraday?" said a voice from a horseback rider to her right.

"Oh! Travis! You scared me! What are you doing?"

"Preparing to ride with you. Hello, Jack!" he said to the driver. "Let me hitch Hero to the buggy, and I'll hop in."

The driver laughed, stopped, and scooted over so Travis could sit beside Beth. Beth was grateful for the twilight. Her face burned. But there was nothing she could do. Making sure her dress was properly draped for modesty, she sat primly and waited for the inevitable. In he came, deftly inserting his great stature in the space to Beth's right. She felt she had suddenly shrunk to half her size.

It was a trip of only a few minutes, but Beth wondered if Travis was as aware of her as she was of him. He looked and smelled wonderful. His tall riding hat, which he had whisked off to get in, topped off as fashionable an outfit as she'd seen him wear. Under a wine wool jacket, a ruffled white shirt rose above a silvery damask vest. Black shiny boots glowed below black trousers that flattered his muscular form and legs.

Conversation between the two was open, yet Beth could not ignore the fact that they sat in the same seat, breathing the same air, touching. Their communication was so satisfying, she wondered if he knew ahead of time the effect it would have.

At the Nugent home, Travis handed Beth out, requested Jack to take care of Hero as well as the other horse, and the driver moved away. Torches lit the path to the house along a flagstone walkway. The flowers Mary had set in the beds were gone now, but it was spring in Beth's heart.

Graham Nugent answered his parents' door. "Travis!" he

exclaimed as he stretched out a hand to him. "Who is this pretty lady with you?"

"Graham, this is Miss Elizabeth Faraday, or Beth, if you're her friend. It was my privilege to meet her on the way, and I begged a ride. We're good friends."

"Well, Miss Beth, I'd say your friend *Trouble* has a bad memory. He doesn't remember that I knew you two when you couldn't stand the sight of each other. You've changed since the days you went fishing at the millpond. You were pretty then, but now you're beautiful," Graham said with a grin. "We're glad to have you here. My mother is right around the corner. May I take your wrap?"

Travis handed him her coat as Mary and her daughter came forward, both smiling. Mary looked lovely in a black wool dress with red trim; and Carrie simply glowed, seeming to outshine her brown and gold plaid. Beth had heard of Carrie's beauty and her happy marriage and, until now, she had thought it a mother's biased opinion. She was wrong.

"It's so good to see you!" said Mary, hugging Beth's shoulders. "Do you remember Carrie?"

"Yes. Hello, Carrie. You look lovely."

"So do you. Travis, you're right. She is special."

Sure her face had not returned to its normal color, Beth caught her breath as another blush radiated. Calm prevailed, though, as she caught a glimpse of Travis's reddened countenance. With a mutual look, both exploded in laughter, and the rest, comprehending the obvious, joined in.

At one end of the long dining room, a great tree covered with decorations and candles attracted the attention of several children. It was the most beautiful tree Beth had ever seen. She felt like a child, too, wanting to examine it for hours.

And so the evening began. To Beth it was a miracle. Not having known a family atmosphere for so many years, she reveled in the love and consideration that poured from the occupants of every room of the house. No one criticized. No one demanded. No one was drinking.

Virgie, in a green striped dress, introduced Beth to the families of Caleb and Joshua. Some of their children were away from school, home for the holidays. Beth found all the Wardens delightful. Inwardly, she scolded herself that, under her father's influence, she had once believed the Warden family beyond contempt. How wrong her father was. Both families represented homes where Jesus lived.

When they were seated for supper, Beth found herself next to Carrie, with Travis and Graham across from them. Before they ate, Riley rose from his place at the head of the table and thanked God for their blessings.

Graham was first to open a subject in which all four were interested. "They're anticipating your arrival at the university, Travis. Are you ready to go back with us?"

Travis's gaze met Beth's. "Yes, I'm eager to begin my medical classes." He looked at Graham and Carrie. "The question is, are you ready to put up with me?"

"Of course we are," said Carrie, her eyes shining. "This is going to be a great year."

Maids started the food around the table, and Beth was thankful. She needed something to take her mind off what had been said. She had refused to think of it before. Now it could not be avoided. Travis would be leaving. He had already told her how much he wanted to be a doctor. It was necessary that he study in Philadelphia, and she had no idea how long he would be gone. She kept eating, but a loneliness that was new to her quelled her appetite.

Later, as they freshened up in a downstairs bedroom, other news lifted Beth's spirits. With happy voices, Mary and the Wardens traded family news and information about each other.

Carrie glanced into a mirror and cleared her throat dramatically. "Since Mama had an obligation with Papa away from the house for a few minutes, I'm going to tell you girls my good news first." She smiled another glowing smile. "After seven long years—"

"Carrie!" Virgie grabbed her sister in a tight hug. "You're in a family way!"

A little tearful, her brothers' wives hugged Carrie, wishing her well. Beth stood aside, happy, yet feeling like an outsider. Obviously Travis didn't know the news, though Beth remembered that the eyes and words of the expectant parents had hinted at their secret all evening.

Last to congratulate her daughter-in-law was Mary. Tearfully she murmured, "I know how you've waited. But this is God's timing, and it's never wrong. He has given Graham time to establish a reputation as a lawyer, and now you own your home. Let's have prayer, girls. I'd like to thank the Lord for this sweet blessing."

All heads bowed, and Mary offered thanks for the baby God would send to Carrie and Graham. She prayed their own Christian lives would influence the child toward Jesus, and she ended the prayer with joy in His name.

Passing single file out the door of the bedroom, the women were startled when Mary suddenly jigged a little dance.

"I'm going to be a grandmother!" she sang, and amid the laughter, Carrie and Mary shared another hug.

❧

For the convenience of the Nugents, Virgie and Conrad took Beth home that night. She saw no more of Travis, so there was no more talk of his going away. She was preoccupied with the thought when she stepped up on the porch at home, and she failed to notice Fred sitting quietly in her father's usual chair.

"Did you have a good time?"

Beth turned and saw her brother smiling. She nodded and smiled, too. "Because you made it possible for me to go, Fred. Where are Pa and Charlie?"

"Pa's in bed. I don't know where Charlie is."

She felt responsible for Charlie, but Pa insisted that she leave him alone. He'd be Charlie's boss, he'd said. She'd already ruined Fred. Still, it bothered Beth that her younger brother ran loose, without discipline.

She returned to Fred's question. "It was an unbelievable evening. Everyone was so nice to me. They were nice to each other, too. I've never seen a group so loving. They all enjoyed being together, Fred, every minute of the time. We had prayer twice, there was a beautiful Christmas tree, and the food was the best I've ever eaten." Beth sat in the other chair near him.

He smiled again. "Sounds like you had a good time, all right. Did you see Travis Warden?"

"Why, yes, he was there."

"I think you really like him, Beth. I know you were with him at the Harvest Festival at church."

Embarrassed before her brother, Beth lowered her head. "We like each other, but I'm not sure we have a chance of being together."

"Because of Pa?"

"That and other reasons. It's complicated."

Fred rested his forearms on his thighs and lowered his voice. "I crept around to the front and listened outside the window that night Travis and Mr. Warden came. I heard them beg Pa to help them, and then he threatened them. Is that the complication?"

Weakly, Beth clasped her hands to her chest. "Yes." She looked into his eyes. "I'm sorry you're in this, Fred. I didn't want you to know about Pa."

"You can't hold all of this inside yourself. It's right that we both know. We need to stay together. You might need me."

Standing, Beth walked to the porch post. "Travis is going away. He's going to Philadelphia to school," she said, trying to act as if it didn't matter.

"I thought he already went to school in Baltimore," he said.

"He did, but he's going to be a doctor. He has to go to the University of Pennsylvania. He's going back with Graham and Carrie Nugent to live with them."

Seconds passed. "Bet you'll be lonesome." His sympathy was real.

"I don't know how it's going to turn out, Fred. I'm just praying."

Fred leaned back in the chair. "I guess prayer helps if you know there's Someone listening."

Beth turned and walked to him. She smoothed his straight brown hair with her palm. "Someone *is* listening, Fred, to every word I say to Him. I believe it with all my heart."

eleven

Only one more day until Christmas. The handkerchiefs for Mary and Virgie and her sisters-in-law were done. Beth had tatted a lace border for each of them and stitched a neat design in the corners. She and Virgie had created special colored paper to wrap smaller gifts in, and ribbons they had made would decorate them.

She had only one day to finish the black satin watch fob she was making for Travis. Everyone else was in bed, and she took the gift out of her sewing basket to work on it. His gift must look exactly right. She was taking special care with the weaving and with every stitch.

"What's that you're doin'?" her father's voice slurred. Hanging onto the door like a serpent ready to strike, he spat, "Answer, girl!"

Stumbling forward, he swatted at Beth but missed and struck the sewing basket. Contents flew across the room, and the shiny watch fob with its black satin attachment lay in full view.

"What's this?" he screeched. Miraculously, he made a dive at the gift and grabbed it before she could get there. "A little gift for somebody, eh? I heard about you goin' round with the son of that devil. Here's what I think of your gift."

Sid grabbed her scissors and viciously slashed into pieces the gift she had worked on for weeks. Crying, Beth gathered up the sewing supplies strewn around the room.

Fred appeared in the doorway, but there was nothing he could do except stand aside. Charlie was still asleep. Panting from his rare burst of energy, Sid stumbled back to the door.

Then he turned and barked a command.

"Get your belongings and get out of here! Go live with your rich, churchgoin' friends. You've turned on the family, tryin' for something better, but the joke's on you. Yer goin' down with the rest of 'em. You don't deserve to live here. We're too good for *you*. Get out!"

"Pa, you can't make her leave." Fred tugged at Sid's night-shirt sleeve. "It's dark night out there and cold. Where will she go?"

"What do I care? I worked all my life for that family and got nothin' for it. Now that I've got the power to turn things around and make us rich, she goes off with the Warden kid behind my back. If she's gone, we'll be better off."

He lunged out of the room, nearly knocking Fred down, and her brother came to her and put his arms around her.

"I can't let you go, Beth. Don't pack. I'll talk to him. Maybe I can change his mind. There's no place for you to go."

"I think Mary will take me in until I figure out what to do. Can you walk me to the Nugents' house?"

Fred hugged her hard. "Sure I can. I don't care what he thinks. Now that you're leaving, I may go, too. I don't want to stay here without you," he said, his voice breaking.

"You can't leave, Fred. You have to keep your job with Mr. Nugent. Maybe someday, with the little bit we both make, we can find a place to live together." She stuck the modest amount of belongings she had gathered up into a worn pillowcase and went to the door. "There are a few leftovers in the cupboard for morning. Outside of the food I've preserved and what's in the smokehouse, you'll have to look out for yourselves."

"Where you goin', Lizzy?" Charlie came out of the bedroom rubbing his eyes.

"Pa kicked her out, Charlie. She's leaving."

"Who's gonna take care of us?"

"You're thirteen, I'm fifteen. We'll have to take care of ourselves." Fred put on his coat, took the bag from Beth, and opened the front door to leave. "I'm going to walk a ways with her, and I'll be back."

Disbelief shadowed Charlie's face as Beth looked back one last time.

⁂

"Of course you'll stay with us, dear." Mary took the pillow-case bag and gave it to Riley. "Let's hurry and get you into bed so you won't take cold. Riley, will you stoke the fire in the blue bedroom? We'll put her in there."

Graham appeared at the head of the stairs in his robe and slippers. "What's going on?" he said sleepily. "Lizzy, is that you?" Surprise alerted him, and he strode down the stairs. "Is there a problem?"

"Indeed there is. That rascal, Sid Faraday, has put Beth out of her home," Riley stated.

Realizing he might have hurt Beth, Riley risked a covert glance and got Beth's only smile of the night. "I'll have your room nice and warm by the time you get upstairs," the man murmured.

"I'm sorry, Beth. I knew Sid had slipped into a worse state since I left home, but to do this to you is inexcusable. What brought it on?" questioned Graham.

"I think I'll answer that," said Mary. "Beth would be too easy on him. Travis has a developing emotion for Beth, and I think she has the same for him. The problem is, in addition to trying to hide it from each other, they've had to hide it from Sid. Unfortunately, he found out that Travis and Beth have been together more than he can stand. For some strange reason, Sid has always hated the Warden family, even though Mortimer gave him a job. Explain *that* kind of hatred to me, if you please."

"I can't, Mother, but maybe we'd better not pursue it any

further. It's hurtful to Beth, I'm sure."

"Yes, let's all get to bed, and we'll discuss the next option to explore in the morning. But, Beth, I guarantee you will not be going back to the life you've had since your mother passed away." Hugging Beth, she said softly, "I won't allow it."

Mary and Beth prayed together upstairs. Then, in a soft bed in Mary's blue bedroom, warm and well loved, Beth spent her first night away from home in a Christian atmosphere.

❧

The four Nugents were at the kitchen table when Beth came down the next morning. She could tell that she had been the subject under discussion. Why wouldn't she be? How many other people had a homeless stray come begging in the middle of the night? And she wasn't even a relative.

"There you are," called Riley. "Did you sleep well?"

"Yes. I'm sorry I slept so long."

"Think nothing of it," Mary scoffed. "We were hoping you would."

A servant brought her breakfast plate when Mary directed her to a chair at the table. Beth could hardly believe the respect she was being shown. Despite her circumstances, it was delightful.

Graham accepted a cup of tea from the girl waiting table and, turning, spoke to Beth. "It was hard to see my old friend in such trouble last night, Beth. Are you feeling better about things this morning?"

"Yes," she said, frowning. "A good night's sleep helped, but nothing's changed. I still have the same problems."

"We'd like to take one problem away," said Mary, wiping her fingers on her napkin. "Riley and I want you to stay with us for a while. When Graham and Carrie go back to Philadelphia, it will be lonely around here. Would you do that for us?"

A tear escaped Beth's eye, and she covered her face with her hands. Finally she murmured, "I know you're inviting me because I have nowhere else to go, but—"

"You're wrong, Bethie," interrupted Mary while Riley made disparaging remarks in the background. "We would have offered before, but there seemed no legitimate excuse to get you away from your father. We care for you and Fred." She sipped her tea and grinned. "Once Jesus gets hold of him, even Charlie has possibilities."

This brought a remark from Carrie. "I want to mention something else, Beth. Mary says the clothes I left here fit you perfectly. Please use them. They're only a couple of years out of fashion, and Mary can help you bring them up to date."

Back went Beth's face into her hands.

"Well, Graham, enough of this," said Riley, relieving Beth of the embarrassment of lifting her red face. "I have a few things yet to do for special customers. If you'd like to come with me, I could use your help."

"Sure. It would be relaxing to work in the shop again," said Graham, and the men left quickly.

"You're all so good to me," murmured Beth. "I can never repay you."

Carrie giggled. "You can repay both of us by using the dresses. Now that you have three or four costumes that are new to you, why don't you decide which one you'll wear to my parents' party tonight? Mary and Riley and all my family will be there. I know we'll have a good time. Graham and I are going out early, and I'll tell Travis you're coming."

"Oh, Mary," Beth moaned, "Pa cut my present for Travis all to pieces. I have no present for him now."

"That's too bad, dear. It was coming along so nicely, too. Let me think what we can do."

"I know something, Mary," said Carrie. "Remember the book Graham looked for the last time we were home and couldn't find? Our pastor gave him another as a gift. Last night I was looking through the shelves in the closet in our room and found the original copy. Wouldn't that be the perfect gift for her to give him? The book would be ideal for Travis and Graham's Bible study together."

"Indeed it would. Do you want it for his gift, Beth? I have a little more paper to wrap it."

Beth moaned again. "Stop! Stop being so good to me. I can't stand any more," she said, her shoulders shaking.

It was very hard to feel bad, though, with Mary and Carrie laughing so hard and hugging her.

❧

Putting on a russet dress that was new to her, Beth's mind reviewed the last twenty-four hours. It was overwhelming. Her life had gone through one change after the other.

But there was so much that was not known. What would her family do without her? How would her father react when he heard that she had actually gone to the Warden home tonight? What would happen to Fred? She had no answers. Only God knew. She knelt by her bed and prayed.

Lord Jesus, thank You for the blessings You have brought to me in such a short time. I'm safe, and I'm with those who believe in You. Thank You, Father.

Dear Lord, please be with Fred. I love him so much, and I want him to find You as his Savior. He needs You. I pray for Pa and Charlie, too. If only they knew how much happier their lives would be if they let You into their hearts.

Be with me tonight. I'm so ignorant about manners and so on. You've been good to let Virgie teach me, but I still have much to learn. If You intend me to be the wife of an educated man like Travis, help me learn, Father. Help me be whole in You and for You. I pray in Jesus' name.

❧

Beth could not account for the welcome she received at the Wardens', so she simply enjoyed it. She felt dearly loved, and no one spoke of her leaving home or the reason she had.

Travis was gone when she first got there, but he dashed in minutes later bearing a package that he stashed underneath the magnificent, luminous Christmas tree. He turned his attention to her, and Beth was sure everyone noticed. She felt her face warm, and the fact that she couldn't keep from smiling assured that the blush wouldn't go away.

"You're here! I'm glad." He took off his coat and hat and gave them to a maid. "Have you had a chance to talk with Mother and Father yet?"

"We chatted when I first got here. As usual, they've been lovely to me, Travis."

He led her to a side table where a maid served them cups of punch. They carried their drinks to a window looking out on the bleak winter, torch-lit night. Travis glanced around the room and lowered his voice to a whisper.

"I heard, Beth. Graham and Riley told me at the shop this morning. I'd like to say I'm sorry, but I'm glad you're out of there."

"My prayers are for Fred. He's respectful of Pa, but it isn't appreciated. Pa takes it as weakness."

"He's a strong young man," said Travis. "I long for him to find the Lord. What a powerful witness he will be!"

"After you talked to him at the festival, I've had several hints that his salvation is on his mind." Beth touched the window frame beside the green velvet drapes. "Now that I'm away, I feel such a burden for Pa and Charlie. They don't realize the value of the new life they can have. They think a believer's life is dull."

"It may seem hopeless to you right now, but we mustn't ever give up. Someone else may break through to them. God doesn't always use the ones who are praying their hardest. Either way, His promises are sure."

They moved through the crowd of relatives—conversing, sampling cider and punch, enjoying the children—and found a sofa in a quieter nook of the living room.

"How do you feel now about helping with the clothing for our friends on the road?" murmured Travis.

"I wanted to do something to help, and sewing is most appropriate for me. It's a skill I can use without leaving home. Your job is the dangerous one." Beth made sure no one was near. "What about Clara's cousin, Travis? Can you tell me anything?"

"No, not yet. I don't see anything happening before I go to school."

A shadow swept Beth's face. "When will you be leaving?"

"After New Year's." He touched her hand. "Will you be sorry, Beth?"

It had come so unexpectedly, she had no breath to answer. She lowered her lashes, and her heart beat wildly. Travis was the handsomest man in the room. His dark green jacket accented his red hair and his broad shoulders. He had asked a question she never thought she'd hear. Raising her head, she started to speak when Gwendolyn interrupted.

"There you are! Come, Beth, we want our special guest to start our line to the buffet. Everyone's waiting." She took the empty cups they held and motioned them ahead.

"We'll continue this later," Travis whispered.

The long dining table bore its delicious burden on a covering of embroidered white linen. Though Travis's remark stayed in her mind, the heavenly fare captured Beth's attention for the next hour. After dinner there was no chance for a personal conversation. The huge, sparkling Christmas tree called, and children responded, noisily begging for presents to be given out.

Beth had never participated in such a celebration. She found herself seated next to Travis and was the focus of attention. Her little gifts to Mary and all the Warden ladies were examined with pleasure and compliments, and Beth received a gift from each family. Later, the reason Travis was late for the evening was revealed.

He presented Beth with a leather-covered Bible. "I had to send to Baltimore for it, and it came late today. That's why I wasn't here earlier." He captured her grateful gaze. "Do you like it, Beth?"

She turned, misty-eyed. "Oh yes! I love it. Thank you."

One of Caleb's children plunked a present in front of Travis. The gift was similar to Beth's in appearance, but unlike hers, the wrapping was ripped away instantly without regard for its use on other holidays.

Travis was pleased with the study book. "It's exactly what I wanted. You see, Graham has one like this. I looked at it in Philadelphia and wished I had a copy."

Mary and Carrie smothered giggles behind their hands, and Beth had to tell the truth. "I confess, Travis. This is a copy Graham thought was lost, and they were given a new copy. Carrie found this one yesterday in a bookcase in their bedroom. We all thought you'd like it."

He thanked the ladies concerned. "Very clever, and I'm extremely grateful."

With carol singing and time dedicated to the reading of Jesus' birth from the Gospel of Luke, the evening came to a close. But Travis had other plans.

He approached Mary and Riley. "May I take Beth home? We've hardly had any time to talk."

Mary left the decision up to Riley. He turned toward Beth, waiting nearby. "Is it all right with you?"

She nodded.

"Then it's fine," said Mary. "You just follow behind our buggy. Beth, make sure you button your coat against the night air."

Travis felt as if a great weight had been lifted from his heart. He wanted time alone with Beth on this night of all nights.

They said good-byes, and the women were helped into the

conveyances. Riley started the horses on their way, and both buggies lurched ahead.

"Are you comfortable?" Travis asked. Beth seemed bereft of words and only nodded. "Did you want to come with me?" She nodded again. "Won't you speak to me? Our ride alone will be useless if we don't talk."

"So—so much has happened tonight, I can't say enough thanks. My own Bible and all the gifts, the holiday food, the friendship your family and the Nugents have shown me—the evening was too exceptional for mere words. The Lord has blessed me more than I deserve."

"None of us deserves God's blessings, Beth. I feel blessed just to be sitting beside you. After the way I treated you when we were kids, I think it's a miracle I'm allowed to speak to you," he said somberly. "Remember how I once told you to learn to be a lady? Well, God showed me. He was bringing up the sweetest lady of all in His own way, in His own time."

Seconds passed. Tilting her head with a grin, Beth answered playfully. "Yoo-hoo, sir. Remember me? I know the true story. I liked nothing better than to irritate you. I lived for it."

"But it's changed now. You don't hate me anymore. And I don't hate you," he said, his index finger tracing her cheek. Without a word, he slipped the horse's reins under his boot heel and took her in his arms. His lips found hers, and the dreams he'd dreamed were real. She was like a flower in his arms, fragrant, colorful, alive. Her mouth curved to meet his, and their kiss was an electric moment that seemed to go on forever.

At last, he raised his head. "I'll be gone for a while. Will you write to me? Please say you will." Again he kissed her lightly.

"I will, I promise," she answered breathlessly.

❧

An hour later, Beth opened her new Bible to read. First, she prayed she would read with wisdom and that she would concentrate on the person and presence of Jesus Christ. The volume felt almost warm in her hand as she thought of the man who had given her the priceless gift.

She was in love with Travis Warden. Regardless of what her father thought of the Wardens, the family had treated her like a beloved daughter after *he* had ordered her out of her home.

Should her father catch Travis or Mortimer Warden in an unguarded moment, he would run screaming to the authorities, and imprisonment for the Wardens was a possibility. She ended her prayer by begging God that it would never occur. But her choice was clear. If her father did make trouble for them, she would stand by Travis and his family.

twelve

During the week between Christmas and New Year's, Beth and Travis saw each other on an almost daily basis. Now both families prepared to go to a New Year's Eve watch party at their church, and despite the fact that Travis was leaving, Beth was determined that every minute with him be a happy one.

Carrying the ingredients to the cabinet to make a cold vegetable dish for their early supper, Beth began a spicy marinade for the plate. Mary busied herself cutting out biscuits from batter on her breadboard.

"Anybody home?" called Graham when he and Carrie came in the front door. "We're later than we thought we'd be."

"We did an errand for Riley," said Carrie. "That's why we're late. I'll wash my hands and set the table."

Mary gave her a quick kiss on the cheek. "Thank you, dear."

Her daughter-in-law moved to a china cabinet in the dining room, and Graham pulled out a chair from the kitchen table.

"I need to talk to you two." Mary and Beth stopped working. Graham's voice told Beth what he had to say was important. "When he came in to work this afternoon, Fred had a bad bruise on his face. His father had hit him."

Hand at her mouth, Beth gasped. Mary wiped her hands and moved to comfort the girl.

"How is he? Was that his only injury?" questioned Beth.

"He said he was all right. Sid was drunk. He hit Fred and Charlie both. Charlie lit out, and Fred hasn't heard from him yet." He eyed his mother. "Travis put ice on Fred's face, and it took down some of the swelling. They're both out in the buggy now, but I thought I'd better warn you. Fred doesn't look too good."

"Bring him in, Son, bring him in. He can stay here," said Mary, finishing the bread and rinsing her hands.

Carrie came to the kitchen door. "We'd like to take him back to Philadelphia with us, Mary. He can share Travis's room. You want him to get away, too, don't you, Beth? Maybe Graham can help him find a job like the one he's doing for Riley."

"May I see him? I want to see how bad he is, and then he can decide what he wants to do." Beth moved toward the hall as Travis opened the front door. "Oh, Fred!" she cried as she ran to her brother. "You look awful. Does it hurt terribly? I'm so sorry."

"Let him sit down, Beth," Travis reminded.

Mary led the way to the parlor, picked a soft chair for him, and set a pillow at his back. "Would you like a cup of my cinnamon tea, Fred? It's your favorite."

"No, ma'am. Thank you. I'd just like to talk to Beth for a while."

"Of course. We'll be in the kitchen," said Mary.

The four left the room, and Travis closed the door behind them. "While they're talking, hear me out," he said. "Riley says Fred's a good worker, Graham, and he doesn't want to lose him. Why don't you let me take him to our house? He'd be welcome, and we have plenty of room."

Mary cleared her throat as she added another stick of wood to the kitchen stove. "Travis, consider what you're saying. Do you really want a guest in the house who's not related to your family?"

"Don't talk in riddles, Mother. We know," said Graham.

The stove lid clattered when it fell from the lifter in Mary's hand. "I'm not sure what you mean," she said hesitantly.

"We know about my father-in-law's activity. And yours, Travis. Not only do we know, we commend you. The trouble is, I don't know if I can keep you two safe from the law."

Travis slid down into the chair opposite Graham. "I can't deny I'm surprised that you know. Maybe it's just as well. Beth has been upset. The greatest danger to us is from her father. He was lurking around the house the night I was drawn into the operation. There was an injured man to be taken care of. Sid says he won't contact the authorities 'for a while.' We don't know what that means, but I'm sure he intends to make the most of his power."

Graham smiled. "The fact that you couldn't resist helping an injured man says you're headed for the right profession. The university should be honored to have you, Dr. Warden." Leaning forward, he lowered his voice. "Tell us where Beth stands on this."

"In the middle. She's torn between wanting to help and apprehension that her father will actually report us. She's sewing with Mother and Virgie, making supplies. But Sid still has the upper hand. Fear of what he may do hovers over Beth like a black cloud."

A frown creased Travis's forehead. "To tell you the truth, I'm not sure I should be leaving right now. Father may need me, and Beth—"

Mary stepped to his side. "Beth will be fine. Riley and I will take care of her. You go on. Get your schooling. Your whole future depends on it."

"You're right, Mother. He's lined up for his studies, and he should go on," Graham agreed. "You can come back if you're needed, Travis. I know the people who can help you travel quickly if it comes to that. Have you ever talked to your father and mother about this? What do they think?"

"Father says the station was in operation long before I found out, and he can keep it going." Travis shook his head hesitantly. "He's absolutely fearless. He sees it as his Christian duty. That's the way I see it, too, but"—he raised his head—"he's Papa. And I love him. I'm afraid for him."

"Cross that bridge in its time," said Graham. "For now, take your father's advice. Go back to Philadelphia with Carrie and me."

Sighing, Mary drew out a long pan from the cabinet for her biscuits. "My concern at the present is for Fred. How can we help him?"

Before she got the answer, the door burst open, and Beth appeared, smiling. Though her eyes were misty, she didn't seem sad. She motioned them to the parlor.

Jubilantly, she cried, "Fred has been saved! He asked Jesus to come into his heart!"

His face wet with tears, Fred sat with bowed head. The rest surrounded him with congratulations and good wishes.

Travis was almost as happy as Beth. It was what they had prayed for. No matter what was ahead, Fred would get through it with the grace of the Lord, and they would all help the boy.

"Tell them, Fred," Beth urged. "We're among friends, people who have prayed for you, and they want to know." She handed him a handkerchief from her apron pocket, and he wiped his eyes and nose.

Finally he began. "First off, Pa didn't go to work. Seems like he's been drunk a lot since Beth left. He. . .he lost his temper, and Charlie and I got out of there. Charlie outran me 'cause my head was making me dizzy. At the shop, Mr. Nugent had me rest, and I think I slept."

Fred seemed set apart when he spoke again. "All of a sudden, I felt Someone was with me, protecting me. I went over in my mind what had happened. Charlie and I could have been hurt a lot worse, but we got away. I remembered Beth telling me how she always felt Jesus near her, and I felt like He was near me, too. I said, 'Jesus, if You're there, I want You to come into my heart.' "

Fred smiled a lopsided smile. "The next thing I knew, He did! It was the best feeling I ever had, and I knew how Beth had felt. I was so happy, I told Him thank You! Then Mr. Nugent and Mr. Travis brought me here so I could tell Beth."

Travis tried to ignore the sweet smile on Beth's face as tears of happiness mixed with a smile. He wished he could take her in his arms, but that would come later. Right now, Fred needed a place to stay.

Mary had a different agenda. "I expect you're hungry, Fred. We'll be eating in a few minutes. Later, the rest of these people are going to a New Year's Eve play party at church, but I'm staying home. Beth, I want Fred to stay here tonight, too. Graham, you get Dr. Winstock to come by here on his way home. I'd like him to take a look at Fred to be sure he's all right."

"I'll go right now," Graham said, leaving no room for Fred to oppose his mother's request. Resettling his hat on his head, he kissed his wife and left.

❧

"And third place for the spelling match is awarded to Eugene Ford!" announced Pastor Thomas.

Applause from the church congregation finally died down, and the three children carrying red, white, and blue ribbons hurried proudly back to sit with their parents. The evening was winding down, and Beth poured two cups of chilled cider for Travis and herself. Making their way through the crowd, they found a place to sit together. It was one hour until midnight.

"The food is still laid out. Would you like a piece of cake or pie?" offered Travis.

"No, but get something for yourself, and I'll wait here until you get back."

He shook his head, sipped his cider, and examined her face.

Beth brushed at her cheek. "Travis, you're looking at me so hard, you're making me nervous."

"I'm memorizing your face. I'm going to be gone for a long time."

"Travis. . ."

"I wish Fred could have been here," he said, looking out over the heads of the other revelers. Beth knew he'd changed the subject deliberately. "He would have liked this," Travis continued. "Now that the pastor knows he's accepted the Lord, he'll be looking for him on Sunday."

"We'll be here. I can't wait to walk in with my brother." Beth let out a deep breath. "Oh, Travis, God has blessed me so since I gave my heart to Him, I have to pinch myself to prove I'm not dreaming. Tonight, for instance, when Riley suggested we fix up that little back room at the shop for Fred, I could have kissed him. With all of us working at it, Fred will soon have a warm, snug place to stay."

"It was a good idea. And with you at the Nugent home, you can see each other every day."

"Tell me the truth. Do you think Pa will leave us alone?"

"I wish I knew. I'm almost afraid to leave, but if we don't trust God to handle our problems, our faith is empty. Beth, you realize that our. . .my future depends on my going away to school. Graham and Carrie leave tomorrow, and I must go with them. Graham has to go to court on Tuesday."

"I know, and I wouldn't have you change anything for my sake. I *want* you to go to school. I'm looking forward to your letters, telling me all you're doing. It will be so exciting for me."

The hour slipped by, and with a shout from outside the building, a sudden boom from a cannon no one knew existed set off the midnight celebration. Whistles, shouts, the beat of metal spoons on washtubs and dishpans, and a gunshot now and then perforated the silence of the next five minutes.

The couple ran outside, and Beth covered her ears against the noise. Someone's baby cried, but most of the children ran in circles, enjoying being able to scream at the tops of their lungs. Beth had never seen a group have so much fun.

Virgie and Conrad approached. "What a commotion!" said Virgie, giggling. "It gets louder every year. I don't know where they got that cannon, but I'll bet they had to lug it in from miles away."

"The evening's been fun," said Travis. "I wish Beth's brothers could have been here. The best times to be had are when believers get together."

Conrad agreed. "I'm sorry about all your grief, Beth. But Fred's a Christian now, and he's in good hands with the Nugents. Maybe you can find Charlie soon and bring him around. Don't you give up."

Beth shook her head. "Charlie's independent. If he wants to come to Fred and me, he'll come. If he doesn't, nothing I could say would make a bit of difference."

❧

Thirty minutes later the families noisily parted. Carrie and Graham went home with the Wardens to spend their last night. With words to the crowd both sentimental and jesting, Riley took Travis and Beth to his house, where Travis had left his buggy.

The three went in quietly and found Mary asleep, her Bible in her lap, in a neat layback chair Riley had created. Their slight movement into the room awakened her.

"There you are," she said, getting up slowly. "Did you all have a good time?"

Beth laughed as she took off her coat. "We had a good, noisy time! Didn't you hear?"

"No, I went to sleep before it started. I did hear something that sounded like a cannon going off. I'm sure I was dreaming."

"You weren't dreaming, my dear," said Riley. "No one knows where, but someone did shoot off a cannon. All kinds of crazy things are happening tonight."

"Come with me, and I'll show you the craziest, but nicest, thing of all."

All three came to attention, and Mary motioned them toward the stairs. With a silencing finger to her lips, she led them to an upstairs bedroom across the hall from Beth's. Opening the door quietly, she stepped back so that Beth could see into the room.

In the glow of a small night lamp, Beth peered across at the bed. Fred slept soundly, his bruised face in full view, and beside him, Charlie lay sleeping peacefully. Pressed close to Fred, he looked the complete picture of innocence whose changed life had taken away his fierce independence and substituted a trace of. . .what? Beth couldn't identify the emotion.

Mary closed the door, and Beth, with grateful, questioning eyes, waited for the lady to speak. All four crept back down the stairs.

"He came to the back door tonight. His bruises are not as bad as Fred's," she directed to Beth. "I knew you'd want to know that. He had something to eat, and as soon as he had washed, I took them up to the bedroom. Charlie was very tired, and he started to cry.

"Fred did the sweetest thing. He put his arm around him and said, 'Charlie, I know Someone who will keep you from being scared the rest of your life.' And he told him about Jesus. I sat back and marveled. I've seen new believers win those they love to the Lord before, but never sweeter than this. Charlie asked the Lord to come into his heart, and we all knelt and said a thank-you prayer.

"I knew God had me stay home tonight for a reason, but I never dreamed it would be for Charlie. Wasn't the Lord good to me?"

Looking at Mary's pleased expression, Beth felt she was, indeed, standing in the reflected glow of Jesus' love.

❧

Riley left to give instructions about the need for a conveyance to the coach stand in the morning, and Mary left Travis and Beth alone in the parlor.

"I'll be in the kitchen if you should happen to want me," she said, leaving the door open to the hall. "I put an extra comforter on the end of your bed, Beth."

"Thank you. I'll be in as soon as I say good-bye to Travis," she said.

Mary moved toward Travis in apology. "Oh, Travis. This has been such a different day, I'm not thinking normally. You're leaving, and I almost let you get away without telling you how proud I am of you. I'll be staying with the boys in the morning, so I won't see you off."

Travis took the hands she extended. "The way you feel means more to me than you know, Mary Nugent. If we hadn't said all this, I'd still know that you're behind me, encouraging my service to God. When I see you, I see Jesus."

He kissed her cheek, and Mary, waving off the compliment, walked back to the door.

"Travis, that's so true," said Beth. "When we see Mary, we see Jesus. What more could believers desire than to be seen that way? I might have known she'd want to stay with Fred and Charlie."

"You're that kind of lady, too, Beth."

Beth raised her eyes to a look of affection that stunned her. She smoothed her upswept hair with a trembling hand.

"I don't know what to say. You took me by surprise. But you're the one to be admired, Travis. I'm nobody."

Travis took her forearms to make her stand still. "Look at me, Beth." He captured her gaze. "You are a child of God. He made you perfect. Read Psalm 139. You can't deny your worth after reading those verses. As you grow older, you will become a stronger believer and a stronger person. We both will."

He let her go, and for a moment she felt she would fall. This was her first test of being without Travis. While she rejoiced at Fred's and Charlie's salvation, the loneliness she would suffer after tomorrow was setting in, and it was devastating. Her brothers would be there, but no one could take Travis's place. She was in love with him.

The feeling seemed to transmit to Travis, and he stepped forward and took her in his arms. Beth raised her head, and her arms went around his neck. She was ready, eager, to receive his kiss. When he let her go, they were both trembling.

"Beth, think how it will be after I come home. I know it's a long time to wait, but we can do it. Please stay true to me, write to me, remember how we are together. Will you do that? I can do anything if I know you're there for me."

Her tears were close. "I have so much faith in you, Travis. I believe you can be a doctor—a great doctor. I'll write you and support you however I can. Just tell me what to do."

He kissed her again. "Grow in God, and help your brothers grow. Everyone will help the three of you stay independent of your father. But pray for him, Beth. Pray that seeing all his children turn to the Lord will make his heart call out for salvation."

"We will. I promise."

Then he was gone. Tomorrow, he, Carrie, and Graham would take the coach to Baltimore, and from there they would catch the train for Philadelphia. There would be no more private time to hold him to her heart and say words

like those they'd exchanged tonight. It would be a dreadful
good-bye, when she would have to hold back tears, say only
that heartbreaking word, and not look at Travis with love.

thirteen

Travis arrived at the University of Pennsylvania with the mind-set of a man with a dream but with the energy of an extraordinary workman. Word of mouth brought students he had met during the summer flocking to him, and because of his dedication, he fit easily into the mainstream of medical study. Motivated by men whose goals were his own, Travis determined that God's call would receive only excellence in return.

He wrote Beth right away to impress her with facts he'd learned about the school. A physician named John Morgan had founded the school of medicine. Morgan had earned his medical degree at the University of Edinburgh, and then included London's city hospitals as an integral part of his studies.

After Morgan introduced it, other medical schools in America followed the University of Edinburgh structure. Although established as the outstanding medical school in the United States, the University of Pennsylvania was unique in that it stressed students' academic ties. It operated within an institution of higher learning. In his letter, Travis wrote:

> Beth, the university had an ingenious founding faculty. They implemented bedside teaching along with their medical lectures. God is so good to send me here. I can't express how excited I am by all that's to be learned at this great university.
>
> Eleven years ago a new organization called the American Medical Association was established, and they named

*the Professor of Medicine at the University, Nathaniel
Chapman, as their first president. The idea is to get every
doctor into the organization for the betterment of the
profession. Think of what it could mean to us all!*

*There's so much more to be learned, Beth. In Europe they
are far ahead of us. We need to press on, to let God expand
our minds. Methods we've yet to dream of regarding the
brain, eyes, and skin, to name a few, are waiting to be
discovered. And there is so much more.*

*You can see now why I'm enthusiastic about being here,
although I wish I could see you every day. Surely you know
my affection for you grows with each week that passes. I tell
myself we must wait until I finish my medical degree. But
when I remember how beautiful you looked the day I left, it's
difficult to hold on to that thought.*

Travis hoped Beth understood. Their future took first
consideration. He and his father had gone over the business
of his financial standing before he had left for Philadelphia.
At the present he could give Beth a home and take better
care of her than she had known before, but his parents
underwrote that life.

He wanted to carve out a life of his own. He wanted to
be God's instrument to heal those both in physical and in
spiritual need. With Beth at his side, they'd make a difference
in the world no matter where or how long they lived.

૨૦

Beth did understand. She, Mary, and Virgie worked silently
before a fireplace in Gwendolyn's sewing room, finishing
work shirts for needful fugitives on the Underground Railroad. The quiet allowed Beth time to reflect on the letter she
had received from Travis. Before they started, she had read
all but the personal section to the other ladies, who were
eager to listen.

In her part of the letter, she seemed to hear Travis's soft voice whispering his dreams for them and for their future. In Beth's *borrowed* world, hard as she tried, it was almost too much to grasp. She had faith in Travis, but to imagine herself the wife of a Christian doctor seemed the height of egotism.

When she let herself, she wished for it, and as she finished the hem of a shirt she had completed, she allowed the idea to wash over her like the music of a well-loved hymn. Taking care of Travis, in a beloved home of their own, while he went to school—what? What put that in her mind? She had promised she would wait until he came back. There were no plans to be together before then.

But as she contemplated those dismal years, she wondered if God had given her a new idea for the future. If they could find a way to make a living, they could marry, and she could make a home for Travis while he studied and learned to be a doctor. Then he wouldn't have to live with Graham and Carrie at a time when Carrie needed more rest. Beth felt she had turned into a good seamstress. Maybe she could sew for people. Maybe—

Gwendolyn appeared at the door with a tray holding a tea service, and laying aside her work, Mary rose to help her.

"Oh, that looks good, Gwendolyn. Just what we need."

Virgie folded her garment and set it aside. "Good, Mother. You had Rosie bake blueberry tarts. Thank you!"

Gwendolyn chuckled. "Now when have you known me not to come up with blueberry tarts when I know you're going to be here?"

Virgie gave her mother a kiss on the cheek, and Beth felt a familiar warmth toward the two women. She was beginning to love Travis's family in a way she had not known before being absorbed into their lives. Another of God's blessings.

Mary opened a cedar chest at one side of the room and proceeded to pack the garments they had been sewing into it. "Hand me yours, Beth. We'd better substitute some fancy work for these things in case the wrong servant wanders in."

"Yes," said Gwendolyn. "I'm sure they all know we do this chore, but you never know when one might decide to turn against us."

Beth ducked her head while setting the bag containing her crochet work, the needlecraft Virgie was teaching her now, in an obvious display by her side. She took the cup of tea Gwendolyn offered and tried not to let her hand tremble.

"We made you uncomfortable, didn't we?" asked Virgie at her side. "Try not to think of what might happen *if.* Some risks are worth taking, Bethie. If someone asks for help, we women do what we can. The rest is up to those who can physically assist him. But to tell you the truth, I wish I were able to help more than I do. I wish I could help Clara Watts's cousin, for instance."

Gwendolyn moaned softly. "Don't say another word, Virgie. Someone might hear and cause trouble. It's too close for comfort just now."

"What do you mean?" asked her daughter. "What has happened, Mother?"

Gwendolyn's glance swept the room, and her shoulders drooped as she whispered to the ladies listening for the explanation. "There's been another accident. Clara Watts's cousin is here. Tar—that's his name. His master gave him that name as an insult to his race. He came from a boat last night, and they could hardly get him here. Your father and one of the other conductors were up nearly all night with him. Mortimer won't let me help when they're bad."

"What can we do, Mother? How can we help?"

"There's nothing to do right now. Mortimer and the slave are both asleep. When they got him patched up, they needed rest. After he wakes up, your father will let me know what to do. I'm nervous about the new girl in the kitchen, though.

She's very. . .watchful."

Virgie's tea sloshed over the side as she set her cup clumsily in the saucer. "One of you can finish my shirt. Mother, I'll borrow the girl for the next day or two until this man is sent on his way. Beth, don't come to my house until I let you know."

Mary set about helping Virgie gather up her belongings. "That's a good idea. Beth and I will stay today and help with food and so on. We can come back tomorrow, too."

"You've taken a worry off my mind, Virgie dear. You always come to the rescue. And so do you, Mary. What would I do without you three?"

A happy smile brightened Beth's face just to be among those mentioned. The women had turned her life of squalor into one under the command of the Savior. She'd returned only a measure of the gratitude she felt.

Gwendolyn and Virgie left to appeal Virgie's case to the kitchen maid, and Mary and Beth settled back with their tea.

"Beth, I wanted to tell you that Fred and Charlie are becoming indispensable to Riley at the shop. I knew you'd want to hear that. And though the boys also seem to think it inevitable, we've seen nothing of your father trying to contact them."

"I'm glad they're being useful to Riley. You've been so good to the three of us. I don't know how we can ever repay you."

Mary reached out and patted her arm. "We want you to grow in the Lord, Beth. Our evening Bible study is helping us all. I expected Fred to enjoy it, but Charlie is beginning to show more interest by asking questions. Who knows? Maybe *he'll* be the preacher someday."

Chuckling, Beth trailed a forefinger around the edge of the china cup. "Oh, Mary, who would have believed a year ago that such a suggestion might be possible?"

"With God, anything is possible," Mary replied. "But why

do I get the idea that you're thinking not only of Charlie and Fred but of someone else?"

Beth set down her tea and covered her crimson face with her hands. Finally she raised her head. "I admit it. I was thinking of Travis. What would the Wardens say if they knew I daydreamed about being married to Travis?"

"I think they'd be honored. You're a Christian girl whose character is excellent, and you're pretty, energetic, and ambitious for Travis. I've seen how he reacts to you," she murmured. "You have faith in him, and it shows."

"I do, Mary. He's going to be a wonderful doctor because the desire comes from his heart. He has a God-given gift." Beth leaned against the back of her chair and sighed. "But there's such a difference in our upbringing. Travis has traveled and had a good education, and I've been nowhere and had no education at all."

"You've educated yourself, Beth. Travis has told me about the discussions you've had. At times, he says, he's had to look things up to carry on a conversation with you that's satisfying. And considering the length of time you've been a Christian, your understanding of scripture is amazing. You must stop thinking of yourself as an uneducated girl. You're far ahead of every girl your age that I know."

❧

The handler had brought Mary's buggy to the front door, and she and Beth were going down the steps when Gwendolyn rushed out the door to stop them.

"Don't go! I need help," she whispered, and at her direction all three hurried into the house and then to the kitchen.

Beth saw a basket full of bloody white cloths sitting on the floor and stood openmouthed as Gwendolyn and the cook dumped them into a tub of cold water. Mary didn't need an explanation.

"Where do you keep the irons, Gwendolyn?" asked Mary,

and at her answer, she took four flatirons out of a closet next to the door and set them on the stove. "Now, Beth, you get rid of our coats and set up the ironing board. As soon as we get these washed clean and wrung out, you'll need to start ironing them dry."

Tub after tub was carried to the back door to be dumped until the bandage material was scrubbed clean. Gwendolyn and Cook hung the cloths on a line stretched across the kitchen near the cookstove. Beth ironed the first stack dry, and then the women took turns ironing the material to renew its cleanliness.

The back door opened, and Mortimer slipped quietly inside. Gwendolyn looked up anxiously from the tub she was cleaning.

"You look so tired," she said. "Is he going to be all right?"

"I don't know, Gwen," said Mortimer. "I wish Travis were here. He has such an instinct about healing. The man has fever. He can't go on. We'll need to keep him for a while."

"Then we will!" said Gwendolyn.

"What about the rest of you? Are you willing to take the chance? Someone may guess and report us."

Beth looked at Mary and Cook. Both were nodding. Those were her feelings, too.

"Then we need to get the doctor and get his temperature down. Mary, may I use your buggy to fetch him?"

"Let me get the doctor," said Mary. "You stay here and do what needs to be done. Beth and I will do the running."

Soon the two were bundled up to leave, and the handler was back at the front door with the buggy. The horses stamped their feet and snorted, their exhaled breath turning to fog in the bitter evening. Mary accepted the reins from the handler and set the team off in the direction of the settlement.

At the doctor's home, Mary guided the buggy to a lean-to shed at the back of the house.

"Beth," she said, "go tell the doctor it's me, and ask him to bring his bag for a trip to the station. He'll understand. Hurry now."

Beth hurried, wondering what to tell the doctor's wife if she happened to answer. She knocked at the door. To her relief, the doctor opened it immediately.

"It's me, sir, Beth Faraday. Mary Nugent is in the buggy. We need you to come with us to the station."

No sooner was the last word out of her mouth than the man grabbed his medical bag near the coat hook by the door. With a quick call to his wife in the kitchen, he followed Beth out the back door and across the yard to the buggy.

Once on their way, Beth marveled at the cooperation she received with such few words. Like Travis, the doctor had a heart for healing. The color of a man's skin did not matter. She reasoned that many in the village helped fugitives. The Chesapeake area, with its waterways, was ideal as a route to freedom.

They reached the crossroads, and in minutes the Warden property came in sight. Mary guided the team toward the front door, the doctor jumped out, and he made his way out to the vine-covered building in the back. A handler took charge of the team and buggy, and Beth and Mary stepped quickly along the path to the front door.

As they reached the porch, Beth glanced toward the barnyard. Terror struck. As if she expected it, she saw a dark figure huddled against the smokehouse. It moved slightly, and Beth gasped. It was him! Her father! Of all nights, he had decided to sneak out to the Warden home and spy on them!

She touched Mary's arm, but the lady had already seen. "Just keep walking. Go on in."

Beth did as she was told, but fear stalked every step. Suddenly guilt overcame her. If it were not for her, there would be no problem for the people she loved most in the world. Her vindictive father, in this act of revenge, could bring them all to their knees.

Tears started in her eyes, and by the time they reached Gwendolyn in the parlor, Beth was crying.

"My dear, what's wrong?" said Gwendolyn, taking her in her arms.

"You're going to hate me," Beth sobbed. "Pa was hiding, watching the doctor go out to the secret place."

Gwendolyn's face paled. "Are you sure?" she said, searching both faces.

Mary took off her coat. "I'm afraid so. What should we do? I'd think the worst thing we could do is go to the men."

"No, we mustn't do that." Gwendolyn sank into a tapestry-covered chair. "We'll just have to wait until one of them comes in. But I think we must prepare ourselves for the worst."

❧

It was hours before Mortimer and the doctor came in from the hiding place. Cook fed them while the women related the scene involving Beth's father. Beth cried softly.

Mortimer listened to the women, then turned to Beth. "You must dry your eyes, little lady. None of this is your fault. We all knew what was involved in helping this man. We came to a decision long ago to help these poor unfortunates as we could. None of us regrets it. I regret your pa hates me so much the station may close. But I'm responsible, too. I made a lot of enemies before I became a Christian. He is only one of them."

Beth protested, crying, yet Mortimer refused to concur. "What we should do now is pray that nothing comes of this. Dr. Winstock has bandaged Tar's injuries, and Tar's fever has come down some. He is resting. There's nothing to do until he is well enough to travel. Let's pray together that God will protect us, and all will go well."

He held out his hand to Beth, and she clasped it as the others followed suit. Mortimer led them in a heartfelt prayer that God would take them through the dark valley into the light, and Beth's heart murmured, *Amen.*

fourteen

Despite her concern, Beth had her quiet time and went to sleep almost instantly when they got home. She managed to get downstairs ahead of Mary the next morning and had a good fire going in the cookstove when her hostess appeared.

"Beth, you're such a boon to me. This cold weather has made my arthritis act up." She sat in a chair by the stove. "Could you make us some bacon and eggs? I'd like to wrap up in a blanket and just warm myself for a while."

"Good. I'll get the blanket."

Beth was back in seconds. After making Mary comfortable, she sliced bacon off a side of pork and laid it in a skillet to fry. Biscuits were no trouble. She whipped them up and slid them into the hot oven. Preparations took hardly fifteen minutes. While she set the table, Mary greeted Riley, who came downstairs neatly dressed.

"That bacon smells good, Beth. Thanks for taking over. Mary got too much night air, I guess." He turned to Mary. "Are you going out there again this morning?"

"A little later," said Mary gloomily. "Gwendolyn needs our help, Riley."

"Well, I think I'd better go to the shop, tell them what to do today, and come back here. I'll drive, and maybe I can help."

"Can you get away without any trouble?"

"Of course I can, and it will give the men a chance to use their own initiative. I trust them. I see Beth has bacon on the table and eggs ready to come up. Sit right where you are, and I'll fill your plate. One biscuit or two?"

Following breakfast, Beth did dishes and ran errands for

Mary so she could stay warm. Riley brought down the heavy coat Mary needed, plus a pair of sturdy boots to keep her feet warm. Beth dressed warmly, too, and at ten o'clock they were ready to get in the buggy that Riley had brought around.

It was a cold morning. The breath of both humans and animals frosted in the crisp air, as the risen sun had failed to make an appearance. On their way, Mary shared her lap robe with Beth while Beth waited anxiously for the sight of the mound on which the Warden home sat.

Just beyond the crossroads, they passed a large wagon full of sacks of grain from one of the Warden mills. Travis had told Beth about this method of transfer. Inside the wagon bed was a compartment built to hide the fugitives they sent along the Underground Railroad. It was where Clara's cousin would ride from the house to the boat.

A handler took the horse and buggy to the barn when they arrived, and Beth and the Nugents were welcomed inside the front door. Not long after, Beth saw the grain wagon pull into the barn lot. The driver aligned the wagon against a fence, where it would wait for its extra burden.

Gwendolyn and Mortimer led them into the parlor as if it were any ordinary day, but when they were inside and the door closed, the Wardens whispered their excitement in quick voices.

"He's better!" said Gwendolyn.

"In God's will, Dr. Winstock worked a miracle. All has been arranged for the transfer tonight," Mortimer added.

Mary sat in a nearby chair to listen, and Beth took away her hat and scarf with her own things.

"How can we help?" asked Riley.

"Keep a watchful eye out, for one thing," said Mortimer. "I have an uneasy feeling about this move tonight."

"My dear," said Gwendolyn, moving to his side and taking his arm.

"I shouldn't have said that in front of you women. Naturally, there's danger involved in any effort of this kind. We've known it all along. Everything has to be done in the dark of night, and the rest we just have to trust God to bring us through. But Tar will be going. It has been arranged, and the quicker we act, the better chance of his getting away. That's our first consideration."

"Are there bandages to be cleaned?" asked Beth. "I can do that while the rest of you tend to more important tasks."

"Yes," answered Mortimer. "I suggest we men help so it will go faster. We can carry out the water to be emptied."

Riley divested himself of his coat, hat, and jacket. "Let's get started."

❧

Once again the hours produced a stack of clean linen for the hiding place, and Cook served another delicious meal.

"In case anyone at this table is interested, we've heard through the grapevine that Travis may be home at Easter," said Gwendolyn, and all eyes including that lady's turned toward Beth.

Beth nearly dropped her fork, and Mortimer chuckled. "I guess the look on her face answers the question, Gwen."

"Mortimer! What a terrible thing to do!" Gwendolyn's face reddened. "I didn't mean for you to reply. You've embarrassed Beth."

"No more than you're embarrassing her now," said Mortimer, still chuckling.

"Oh! Beth, I'm sorry." She reached for Beth's hand. "We had a long talk about you last night. You've been so faithful, both to Virgie and Conrad, and to the rest of our family, we've grown to love you."

Mortimer cleared his throat and continued the compliment. "We'd like you to know that we hope someday to have you as a member of our family. You and your brothers have proven that honor is in the individual, not in where they come from."

Beth could not speak. Picking up the napkin from her lap, she dried her eyes. Before she was even asked, the Wardens had told her they approved of Travis's selection of her as their daughter-in-law! They understood that her father's manner of betrayal would never be her attitude toward them. She could do nothing to stop him, but she would stand with Travis and the Wardens no matter what came.

"Now that we have established who's in love, let's get on to the business at hand," said Mortimer, rising from the table, and Gwendolyn smacked at his arm and missed. "Riley, go with me to the barn, and I'll leave you there to check on Tar. That would be similar to what we always do. Hopefully no outsider would notice anything amiss."

Once more bundled up in heavy coats, they left the house. Beth couldn't resist peeking through the lace curtains at the shrubs, trees, and buildings surrounding the house. But she saw nothing resembling the figure of her father, and relieved, she exhaled the breath she had been holding. Joining Mary and Gwendolyn before the blazing fire in the parlor, she settled down to pray and wait with them.

❧

At nine o'clock, lamps were blown out from the top to the bottom of the big house. With Beth, the ladies and several trustworthy servants watched Mortimer and Riley make their way stealthily from one shadow to another toward the hiding place. Beth's trembling was uncontrollable now. This was the moment each of them had prayed most about as the evening wore on.

She realized she was as involved as Travis and his family in what was deemed unlawful by the authorities. But so were Virgie and Conrad, the Wardens' sons, the Nugents, Dr. Winstock, and others in the village who believed in freedom as a God-given right. She could do nothing less than her best to help.

Tonight they'd packed some of the garments they had made together with food in a small bag Tar could easily carry. A boat would carry him along the planned route to Bodkin Point. Next was Baltimore, then on northward, from one station to another, until he reached Canada. Beth breathed yet another prayer for his safe arrival.

Suddenly someone pounded on the front door. Beth felt every heart in the group of watchers had stopped.

"Gwen! What shall we do?" whispered Mary.

"Newt, you'll have to answer," Gwendolyn said to the boy who brought wood for the fires.

"Me, ma'am?" he asked, his voice shaking. "I'm too scared. I can't go."

Cook swatted the boy's rump. "You go anyway! Say we're all in bed and you can't disturb the family."

The boy obeyed, moving slowly, followed by the group, to a door leading to the foyer. The others stopped there so they could hear. The front door vibrated with pounding again. Newt stopped, obviously unable to make himself move.

"Go on, Newt! You hear me?" Cook urged in a raspy voice.

The boy approached the door and tugged it open. Through the door, like a whirlwind, plunged a small figure.

"I gotta see Lizzy Faraday! I know she's here! Go get her! I gotta see her!"

Beth stepped out clear of the group. "Clara! Yes, I'm here. What is it?" she said, her trembling turned to panic.

"They're comin', Lizzy! Your pa and the law! They're comin' to get Tar! I heard talk of it awhile ago, and now I know it's true."

Beth grabbed Clara's arms. "How do you know they're coming? What have you heard?"

"My pa overheard some men talking about your pa. They

said that old Sid was in cahoots with the sheriff, and the sheriff's deputized some men in the settlement to come and help him get Tar."

"How would Pa know the sheriff?" Beth scoffed.

"He made him a good story, Lizzy. He went out of his way to send word to the sheriff. And word back says he's comin'."

"Dear Lord, please," Mary prayed.

Gwendolyn grabbed her coat from the hall rack. "I have to tell Mortimer. They'll catch him halfway between the room and the boat!"

"No!" protested Beth. "I'll go. It's my fault you're all in danger. If it weren't for me, Pa wouldn't be so angry with Travis's family. All you've done is be good to me. All I've done is make Pa angrier."

Cook's voice was like a sharp sword. "Too late! They're here!"

Crowding the windows, they watched the unfolding scene. Men straggled from the underbrush and hedges and covered the land surrounding the barn lot and yard. Squirming shadows did a dance of death, created by torches and lanterns the slave catchers carried.

"There must be twenty men out there," said Cook, clearly nervous.

Beth saw Mary press her palm to her forehead. "Think! Think!" the lady said aloud to herself and all. "There's safety in numbers! We all go out. Make them arrest us all: the Wardens, the Nugents, and one little Faraday. Plus they have to take note of the people who work here." She eyed Clara. "You'd better stay inside, dear."

Beth could have shouted, but she said calmly, "It's a wonderful idea, Mary. Let's get our coats. There are handlers in the barn, too. They'll come out. There *is* safety in numbers!"

Three minutes later the group filed out the back door.

❧

"What did I tell you? See there? My own kin in the middle

of the outlaws!" Sid Faraday sprang first one way then the other, striving for everyone's attention as he pranced along.

Beth and her friends marched toward them until they were adjacent to the hiding place, and they stopped. The men halted, too, staring. Their faces told the story. They hadn't expected to be met by a crowd of people coming from a darkened house. In addition, two men came from the barn on their right. Beth thought she saw the bravado slipping away, bit by bit, as the men in the mob counted the number of people they would have to confront.

"What's going on here?" Mortimer's voice rang out over the silent crowd. "Gwendolyn, is that you? What are you and Mary doing out here in the night air? Your bones will be aching."

"I don't know what's going on, dear. These men came stumbling up around the house, and we put our coats on and came out to see what was happening. Can you make it out?" called Gwendolyn.

Beth's father looked as if he would explode. "Listen to me, Sheriff. They're playacting. They're sneakin' slaves through under everybody's nose. They've got one here tonight, gettin' him ready to go. Look around. You'll find him. Go on! It's your duty!"

"I think you'd better cool down and let me handle things, Faraday. We need proof of your charges. So far, I have only your word that Mr. Warden is guilty," said the tall man wearing the badge.

"You get out your gun. He's here someplace. I saw him brought in last night."

"I'll get my gun when it's time. Just settle down until I find out more of the facts." The sheriff's sharp tone told Beth that he, like the rest, had lost patience with Pa.

"Why don't you get to searchin' then? At least do that!"

The sheriff moved toward Mortimer. "We have to search

your property, Mr. Warden. This man says you're part of the route for runaway slaves. That's a pretty serious charge."

"Well, you're welcome to search, but you won't find anything except a mare in foal. Riley and I were just checking on her. Sid Faraday works for me at the mills, but I'm sorry to say he hates me. You see, before I became a Christian, I was not a reasonable man. A lot of people hated me in those days. Although few have carried their grudges as long as Faraday, he has a list of grievances against not only me, but against all the Wardens. Our friends the Nugents, too."

"Is that right, Faraday? Have you got me here because of a bunch of old grudges against the Wardens?" asked the sheriff.

"I gotcha here 'cause I seen what's goin' on. More than once. You search this place, and you'll find what you're lookin' for."

Reluctantly, the sheriff sent several men to circle the house, the barn, and each of the outbuildings. The hiding place was so overgrown with vines and brush, no one was assigned to go there. Obviously no one felt it was significant. No one but Sid Faraday.

"You forgot that building. The one with the vines all over it. Make 'em cut through that rubbish and look inside."

The sheriff's temper rose again. "I'll conduct this search my own way, Faraday. You stay out of it so these men can do their work!"

Sid's temper was out of control. "I'm tellin' you, that's the best place he coulda hid him! Make 'em go look!"

"And I'm telling you for the last time! Get out of here and let me do my job!"

His face contorted with anger, Sid Faraday looked left and right, his mouth in a cruel grimace. Suddenly he leaped forward, grabbed the butt of the sheriff's gun, and pulled it out of his leg holster. Holding the gun over his head, Sid made for the hiding place with the sheriff hard on his heels. Beth broke away from the crowd and followed in horror.

Jerking the door open, Sid pushed it back into the path of the sheriff. The door caught him unaware, and the tall lawman stumbled into weeds surrounding the vine-covered outbuilding. Sid had free rein to ready and fire the gun. Beth couldn't see the man lying hurt inside, but she could see her father. He pulled back the hammer of the pistol and fired. A shrill scream splintered the night.

Beth realized it was she who had screamed. A guttural moan accompanied the gun's explosion. Her pa was a murderer. Quickly, Mortimer and Riley and the group from the house pressed forward. Lanterns lit the scene. The sheriff wrenched the gun from Sid's hand and ordered him held. Mortimer scrambled through to kneel beside Tar.

"Are you all right?" asked Mortimer.

He got no answer.

He took the black man's hand and raised his eyes to the sky. "Please, God, don't let him die. He's never had a chance. All he knows is mistreatment. He just wants to be free of pain and have a decent life. Please, Lord."

Beth prayed, and heads around her bowed, too. When she raised her head, her gaze fell on the slumped, incapacitated body of her pa. Staring at Tar, Sid seemed hypnotized by the sight of his crime. Beth looked back at his victim.

Amazingly, Tar's eyes opened slightly and riveted on the face of Sid Faraday. His lips moved, and Mortimer leaned down to catch his words. When he sat up straight, he turned toward the people outside the room to repeat what he had heard. Tar's eyes closed.

"He said, 'I forgive him. Tell him. . .please, give your heart to Jesus.'"

Beth fell to her knees and felt Mary's and Gwendolyn's arms around her. Confusion gripped all who had seen and heard what went on. It was the worst night of Beth's life. She yearned for the feel of Travis's arms holding her. She heard voices of men nearby, sick with loathing.

"I didn't bargain for this," said one. "I'm getting out of here."

"Me, too," said another, and she heard similar remarks from other men who had come with the sheriff.

Footfalls retreated to the yard and on to the road. The deputized band was breaking up, and the sheriff realized it, as well.

"What a mess!" the tall lawman complained. "One of you bring Faraday along. I'll lock him up and sleep on this before I make a decision. Mr. Warden, will you take care of the body?"

Mortimer, still holding Tar's hand, nodded but did not rise.

"Tomorrow's Sunday," said the sheriff. "We'll get to this on Monday morning."

The next hour was like a nightmare to Beth. The women and those who had come from the house slowly ambled away from the secret place while keeping an eye on the sheriff, his prisoner, and his decreased number. Mortimer and Riley did not go to the house with the rest.

Inside, Clara was next to be dealt with. Beth agonized over what lay ahead. How could she tell Clara her cousin was dead? The two girls had been friends all their lives. Beth found it hard to breathe. Clara's coming grief clutched at her heart.

They seemed to be moving in slow motion as they all took off their coats and head coverings that had warmed them against the cold. Clara was nowhere in sight. Beth reasoned that she would hide until someone found her to reassure her that all was well.

"I'll look for Clara and tell her. She doesn't know if we're friend or foe. I'm sure she's scared to death."

"All right, dear," said Mary. "Bring her in here with us."

Beth turned to leave when the back door beyond the

kitchen opened. Riley stepped inside, strode heavily into the kitchen, and slumped in a chair at the table.

"Is there any tea or coffee?" he said, letting out a weary breath.

"Always," said Cook, and she hurriedly lit a lamp and poured tea from a warmer on the stove.

"This wild night was too much for me, but I can always use a happy ending."

Mary moved quickly to his side. "Riley Nugent, you say what you mean!"

Riley laughed. "I mean, that boy is not dead. He fainted with pain. Tar has an ugly gash along the side of his chest, but he's being well taken care of. Within the hour he'll be on his way to freedom!"

This time the tears in the kitchen were from sheer happiness. Clara was present in time to share the joy.

Mortimer was equally optimistic and equally exhausted when he appeared. He sat with Riley at the table and at first addressed Clara, who stood quietly with Beth at the back of the group.

"Clara, your cousin is going to be all right. As for the rest of you," he said with a wave of his hand, "you did the right thing. I think you scared the sheriff half to death. He didn't know what to do with you all. Beth, I don't know what to say to you. I'm so sorry you were caught up in this. None of it has been your fault, yet you're the one who's suffered most."

"No more than you," Beth said in a tremulous voice. "What happens to you now?"

"I don't know, Bethie," he said with some affection. "Whatever happens, I don't blame you. Nobody can help who they're related to." Mortimer sighed. "The next move will be the sheriff's when he visits me Monday morning. By then he may have learned that some of his own *deputies* were on our side and helped get Tar away."

"The sheriff saw the hiding place."

"Yes, but he struck me as being a man of reason. Maybe he'll listen. First, the sheriff saw Sid at his worst. He must have seen how prejudiced he is. It was obvious that despite the fact that Sid works for me, his main goal was revenge. Next, if we can convince him Tar's life was unbearable, he might not charge me. Last, the army of people congregated here tonight may bring to mind the problem it would be to arrest me without protest."

"That's a fact, Mortimer," said Riley. "If this thing turns out like I think it will, people around here won't like you going to jail for being kind. We'll wait and see what happens, but I doubt the sheriff will be able to make a case against you."

"Just the same," said Mary, "I make a motion we have an on-our-knees prayer meeting here and now."

Beth's eyes closed, and she sank to the floor beside Clara and Gwendolyn.

fifteen

The road from the crossroads whirled with dust whipped up by two horses and their riders. Travis and Graham strained their eyes to catch the first glimpse of anyone stirring at the Warden house.

"I don't see a soul, Graham," Travis exclaimed. "Where do you think they could be? It's almost sunset."

Graham swatted the livery horse with his crop. "We'll have to wait and see. Who's that at the front gate?"

"Beth! How do you like that? The first person I see!"

"That's strange. Wonder why she's out there all by herself?" Graham slowed his horse as they neared the house.

Travis raced ahead, jumped down, and grabbed Beth in his arms. "My sweet girl," he murmured and kissed her repeatedly.

Lost in the ecstasy of Travis's nearness, Beth was speechless.

Laughing, Graham spoke instead. "First things first, I always say, but now that we're here, let's find out what's going on." Graham waved off the handler who was coming across the barn lot at a run. "We'll leave the horses here until we decide what to do. Let's go inside and have something warm to drink. Do we have time, Beth? Or should we head out for the settlement?"

"I have hot coffee on the stove," she said, her gaze hardly leaving Travis's face. "Let's go in, and I'll explain what's happened up to now."

With his arm around her waist, Travis led them up the path to the house. Inside, they divested themselves of their heavier garments and hung them near the door. Beth hurried to the kitchen. Aromatic wisps of steam from the fresh coffee she poured welcomed the tired travelers.

"First, tell me how you got here. I've been patient long enough," she said, returning the coffee to the stove.

"Indeed you have," Graham replied, chuckling. "I couldn't get by delaying an explanation to my Carrie." He set his cup down and relaxed his shoulders. "God did the whole thing, Beth. A Mr. Brown came to me for legal advice. He was making a preliminary visit with the intention of moving his family to Philadelphia, and I handled a certain piece of property for him. Brown had worked with Mr. Abraham Lincoln on his campaign for senator in Illinois last year, and he said Mr. Lincoln had heard of me. Are you properly impressed, Beth?" he asked, grinning.

She nodded, returning his smile, and he continued. "During our conversation, Brown inadvertently dropped a hint that his boss, a federal marshal, was waiting to hear from the territorial sheriff regarding charges allegedly against a man named Warden. Travis and I talked, and we decided the coincidence was too close to reality for comfort, so we set out immediately. Since then, on the train coming here and at the livery stable in Baltimore, we learned we were indeed needed. Word of mouth travels quickly when a situation is critical."

From the first, Travis had watched Beth. He could not get enough of the sight of her. In a high-necked navy blue dress piped with ivory, she sat poised like a princess, listening, her expression one of fervent attention. Her life was being played out before her without her participation, but she was calm and sweet-minded. She was everything Travis wanted for a wife.

He took her hand as he spoke. "Tell us what we need to know, Beth. Start from the beginning."

Her lower lip trembled, but she knew they had to hear. "Pa caused all the trouble. He notified the sheriff, and the sheriff came to the house with a band of men he had deputized. Tar was here, too sick to travel. There were several of us in the house and some in the barn. We all went out at once, and I think it made the sheriff have second thoughts about what to do. But not Pa. He grabbed the sheriff's gun and shot Tar.

"The sheriff took Pa away and said he'd be back today. But at dawn both your parents, with their household help, met together. They planned to canvas the village to see if they could find sympathizers to persuade the sheriff it's a special consideration case.

"That's all I know. They wouldn't let me go with them on account of Pa. I stayed here last night, and so did Clara, but she left this morning. It's been a long day, and I don't know what else has happened. You two do what you feel is right."

Graham rose from his chair. "We'd better go, Travis. They may need me to represent them. Are you ready?"

"Absolutely. Beth, I smell the pot of meat you've been cooking. Do you have enough vegetables to make stew? We don't need dessert."

She smiled. "Yes, and I'll make some corn bread. I've already done some pies. Bring home anyone you please."

Travis caught her hand. *How blessed I'd be to have my darling girl greet me at the end of each day the rest of my life.* Travis thanked God in a brief prayer and asked Him to go with all who needed the Lord's care in that hour.

"The writer of Ecclesiastes says in chapter nine, 'Whatsoever thy hand findeth to do, do it with thy might.' So let's be on our way, Travis, and find out what the Lord wants us to do with our might."

Beth followed to the front door to help them into their coats.

Suddenly, from outside, a distant sound of shouting and merrymaking pierced the chilly air, becoming louder by the second. They threw back the door to a view none of them expected. Carriages, buggies, and riders on horseback lined the road from the crossroads.

A small army of townsfolk tramped to the front gate and let themselves into the yard. Mortimer and Gwendolyn arrived in their buggy ahead of the Nugents, and all made a noisy approach to the front door. It soon became apparent that the people had come prepared to eat, for each lady brought a generous family offering from her larder. Beth, Gwendolyn, and Mary hurried with Cook into the kitchen and dining room to lay out a buffet for the crowd. Guests took off their wraps, ready to help.

Mortimer burst through the flow of bodies but stopped suddenly at the sight of the two Philadelphians. "Travis! Graham! How did you get here? And on such a day!"

"We heard you might need us, so we're here," said Graham.

Mortimer lowered his head in a familiar way, and Beth knew he was thanking God. The noise of the household forced them to move away from the chattering crowd in order to talk.

"It was an amazing day," said Mortimer in a reverent voice. "The sheriff is a Christian man! He talked to many people in the area on Sunday. Now here's the unbelievable part: He came to me after church and showed me a petition the people of the settlement had drawn up, and it was signed by seventy-two people. It was a testimony of my value, my Christian value, to the community. I don't deserve such words after the way I treated people before Jesus came into my life.

"But the sheriff listened to my friends who had signed the petition. Every one of them claimed they had helped Tar get away from his owner and sent him on his way from here alive. Of course the sheriff could never prove that—no more than they could prove they had. For every question, the crowd called out an answer. It soon became an outdoor trial. At last the sheriff said he'd get in touch with me if anything further was needed, but I doubt I'll ever hear from him again."

Travis paid attention to his father's account of the town meeting, yet managed to hold Beth in view the whole time. He had not had a moment alone with her since he kissed her hello, and he wondered if he ever would.

It did happen. After a banquet satiating the appetite of every guest, the company drifted back to the settlement; and Travis found an excuse to walk with Beth to the smokehouse to return a side of smoked meat.

"Oh, Travis, I'm so happy!" said Beth when he'd hung up the meat. "Imagine God sending a sheriff who is a believer! I feel guilty now that I wasn't there with Fred and Charlie. They were brave enough to face Pa."

"I need to tell you about Charlie. Mr. Curtis offered Charlie a job at his general store. He plants a garden behind the building each summer to sell fresh vegetables. He's going to turn that job over to Charlie. Until then, Charlie will help keep the store clean and shelve the merchandise Mr. Curtis gets in. The salary's enough to feed him, and with Fred's job and Riley's fixing up the room in his shop for them, the boys should be able to manage very well. Of course, the church will watch over them, too."

"I'll be sure to thank Mr. Curtis," she said. "But I can't keep from thinking about Pa. He needs the Lord, Travis. Even though they let him go, he hasn't changed. He acted remorseful because he shot Tar, but he hates your father. He could still be dangerous."

A kitchen maid came through the door of the smokehouse to return an unused pail of potatoes. After pouring the potatoes in a bin, she smiled at them and left. The couple followed her out.

When the girl was out of earshot, Travis spoke softly. "Beth, what are we going to do about us?"

He tried to take her hand, but Beth tugged at her glove. "What do you mean?" she asked.

"My love, we mustn't waste time. You know I want to

marry you. I think you want the same thing. If so, we need to speed up our plans. I want you with me in Philadelphia as soon as possible. I have years of study ahead. With you there, I could concentrate on my work better, and you could help me through. You are the helpmeet God meant for me, Beth."

Beth reached out for his hand, and they took a roundabout walk to the house. "I do love you. I want to be your wife. I've prayed God would open a way for me to support us while you are in school. I can sew or even clean for people, Travis. Your sister could help me find people who need that kind of help, and I could repay her by helping her as she gets closer to her confinement."

They had strolled beyond a tall cypress tree, stripped of its foliage by winter storms. Travis tucked Beth's arm under his, hoping the warmth of his greatcoat would block the cold wind impelling them to take shelter.

"I'm not penniless, Beth. I should have made that clear to relieve you of worry. I can afford to support you while I'm in school. We'll be together in a little place of our own. It sounds like heaven to me."

She leaned her head against his arm. "It sounds like heaven to me, too."

"When can we be married, Beth? I have to go back right away, so I know this is too soon. Can you be ready when my classes are over in the spring?"

Beth giggled. "I don't have much to get ready, Travis. But by spring I expect Mary and Virgie and Gwendolyn will have a list of things I must have before we can set up housekeeping. We need to be married here, or people will be hurt because they can't get to Philadelphia to attend."

"You're right," he said, exhaling a long sigh. "I'll just have to manage without you until then. Will you write often so I'll know how things are progressing?"

"You know I will." She raised her head, and slipping her

arms around his neck, she made a new demand. "Now would you kiss me, please, right in front of all those people that I know are watching us from every window on this side of the house?"

Travis needed no further invitation. Pulling her to him, he nestled her head in his hand and captured her mouth with his. Not all their problems were solved, but for the moment he forgot them and kissed Beth with a passion he hadn't felt before. They were in a world of their own.

But not as alone as they thought. From the house came shouts of joy from people who were, as Beth suspected, watching from every window. Some even stepped outside and clapped to encourage them.

Beth buried her burning face in Travis's coat while he yelled at the shivering onlookers to grant them privacy. Grinning, he looked back at the girl in his arms, and, finding her lips, he returned them to their own world.

≈

"Are my girls ready to go home with me?" asked Riley on a Sunday afternoon a month before the wedding. "Gwendolyn, that was a superb lunch. Thank you!" He shook hands with Mortimer. "I need to be available in case the Stanfels get by to pick up their table. He intends to borrow his neighbor's wagon."

"Oh, Riley, I'd forgotten about that," said Mary. "Beth, can you be ready to go right away?"

At her assenting answer, Gwendolyn and Mortimer rose from their chairs in the parlor where the friends had gathered.

"I'm glad you came to lunch with us. Come out next Sunday. We'll make more plans for the wedding," begged Gwendolyn.

Mary laughed. "You eat with us next Sunday. We're eating you out of house and home. We can still plan the wedding. In fact, we need to show Riley what we'd like built for the church altar right away."

Beth stood quietly listening. It didn't matter that it was her wedding; the important thing was that Mary and Gwendolyn were pleased with the process. She and Travis would be satisfied.

Riley lowered his voice to speak to Mortimer, and Beth was reminded of the dark days past. "We thank the Lord every day that a sheriff has some leeway in the cases to be prosecuted. And there's still a chance to bring Sid Faraday to the Lord."

"He still has his job," said Mortimer. "I can't bring myself to deal civilly with Sid like I did before the night of his revenge, but I didn't fire him. That night he spent in jail was enough. They tell me he became a shuddering mass of contrition. Since he wasn't really a murderer, he wasn't locked up for good. But he's changed. He no longer meets his drinking friends at the tavern. He spends his days dismally silent at the mills and then goes home to a lonely house. Doesn't even light a lamp. Twilight sends him to bed," he ended sadly.

Beth heard the whispered conversation with a breaking heart. How could she leave, knowing her father was so lost and lonely? She had to make one last attempt to bring closure to her father's tragic story.

She was dashed from her reverie by a noisy farewell, and soon Beth and the Nugents were in the buggy, the harness jingling as the horse trotted along through the bright, sunny day. Passing through the village brought an occasional wave from a yard or porch, and in minutes Riley brought the horse to a stop in front of their home.

"This has been a quiet ride," said Riley. "Are you ladies talked out?"

"Not really," replied Mary. "I've been taking Beth's measure on the ride. There's something on her mind. Can you spare the buggy if we take a drive?"

Riley was more than amenable, and they went on their way.

The two settled themselves more comfortably in the greater space and spread their skirts to smooth out the wrinkles.

"All right, my dear, what are you thinking? Why are we here?"

Beth chuckled softly. "Mary, I can't hide anything from you. Not that I want to." She set her handbag aside and clasped her gloved hands together. "I'm so burdened for Pa. I'd like to speak to him about his salvation, but I'm not sure I'm the one to do it. I've always been so afraid of him."

"Maybe you haven't trusted Christ to do it for you. It's His power you need. Let Him do it for you, Beth."

They did not speak the rest of the way, and Beth prayed until the house came in view. They found Sid sober and as dreary as they could have imagined. He didn't invite them in, but he didn't stop them, so they went inside and sat on the sofa.

"Guess you came to say you're sorry," he said to Beth. "Heard you're cozy with all my enemies. Ain't you 'shamed?"

Beth prayed a last silent prayer. "No, Pa, I'm not ashamed. I'm just sorry there's been so much trouble between us. But Fred, Charlie, and I have found the Lord. Our lives have changed, and we want yours to change, too. Please, Pa, won't you accept Jesus as your Savior?"

Sid swore. "I don't want to accept Him. No use beggin' me."

"He's the answer to all your unhappiness, Pa."

"I ain't unhappy. I'm fine."

Beth's voice softened. "Jesus died for you, Pa. He was perfect, and He didn't have to, but He took your sins on Himself because He loves you, and He died on a cross in your place."

"What sins? I ain't got no sins. You're the one with the sins."

"That's true. I am a sinner. But He forgave me on the cross, just as He did you."

"I didn't ask Him to do nothin' for me."

"I know you didn't. He did it because He wants you to have eternal life in heaven."

For half an hour he scoffed at, ridiculed, and accused Beth. But she kept on, persuading him to open his mind to the Lord. Mary sat in silence with her head bowed, praying.

Frantically, Sid paced back and forth through the room, at times covering his ears with his hands. His fury burst out in a final rush. "It's no use! You're through!" He yanked the door open and motioned for them to leave. "Get outta here!"

"Pa, please, won't you accept Jesus Christ as your Savior?"

For a moment, time seemed to stop.

"Yes!" said her father, bursting into tears and dropping to his knees as if he had finished a long race and won.

With tears of gratitude, both women knelt with him in prayer. Over and over Beth thanked Jesus for what He had done, and Sid thanked Him, too. They left then, and a different man promised to clean up and come to supper at the Nugent home. It was time for Beth's father to face all his children together.

In the short time she had left with her family, Beth brought them together to focus on their newfound faith. Bible study and prayers for each other strengthened them to build on the precious gift God had given. In a letter to Travis, Beth shared her heart: The miracle of her father's salvation showed how willing God was to keep His promises.

❧

"You'll be the most beautiful bride in the world, Beth," said Virgie, after wrapping a sheet around Beth's bridal gown and hanging it up in her mother's sewing room.

"You certainly will!" said Mary. "That ivory taffeta with your blond hair makes you sparkle like a star. On your wedding day, you'll truly shine!"

Gwendolyn came through the door with a bundle in her arms. "Here's another! Beth, we're going to have to build on an extra room for the wedding presents. This is a quilt, a big one they made at church. It might even do for a bedspread."

She spun out the folded quilt, and the ladies gasped at its plump, multicolored beauty. Beth stroked the blocks of color with a light touch, and Mary noticed her melancholy look.

"What is it, Beth? This quilt has made you a little sad. Why?"

Beth was ashamed but decided to answer Mary's questions. "My mother once had a quilt similar to this one. Pa used it to shelter a rabbit hutch he experimented with one summer. Dogs got after the rabbits, and the quilt was torn to shreds."

Mary put her arms around the girl. "It was a bad memory, dear, but remember the pastor's message this morning. Jesus is the way, the truth, and the life. Your Savior has given you a new life in Him. Maybe He gave you this beautiful new quilt to erase that bad memory."

Smiling, Beth hugged Mary back. "You're right. I know He did." She smoothed the quilt with her fingertips. "If I want to live a life full of Christ, I have to forget my old grudges and trust Him with my future. This quilt belongs to Travis and me, and it will always be precious to us."

❧

"Travis Warden, you go on home now. It will soon be midnight, and you can't see Beth on her wedding day." Mary put the glasses and the dishes of candy and cookies she'd served on a tray, and Riley took it from her and started for the kitchen. "Now I don't call that superstition," she said. "I call it tradition. A bride should look her best for her wedding. Beth needs rest, so"—Mary pointed her finger at Travis— "you! *Go!*"

Chuckling, Travis held out his hand to Beth, and she rose and brushed away a wrinkle in her yellow linen dress. "Looks like I have no choice, darling Beth." He raised his voice. "Do I at least get to kiss her good night?"

Riley yelled back, "Why not? I'm going to kiss my girl good night."

"Riley!" Mary scolded, and the two in the parlor laughed happily.

"Can we walk outside?" asked Travis. "Do you need a wrap?"

"No! You can keep me warm if I need it."

"Gladly," he said and led Beth to the front door. "Everything has been arranged for our trip back. Carrie and Graham are staying another week, so we'll be settled in at our place by the time they get back. My father had all the presents shipped to Philadelphia, and the housekeeper I hired should have everything in place when we get there."

"I can hardly wait. People have been so good to us. It will be wonderful to use all the household goods they've given. They're all so special and colorful. And my *trousseau*, as Virgie calls it—and partly because of her—is beautiful. I think you'll be proud to introduce me to your friends."

Travis put his arm around her and drew her close. "I've been proud of you since I realized what a mule I was to keep fighting with you." He brushed a strand of blond hair from her forehead. "God has brought our dreams to fruition, my love, and tomorrow we'll start our new life together. I have a lot of work ahead, but now that I have the one I love to share it with me, the days won't be so lonely."

Leaning against his chest, Beth slipped her hand up to his cheek. "When we meet tomorrow, we will be one in Christ. How the Lord has blessed us, Travis, to work out our lives and bring us to this day. My love, let's have prayer before you go."

They closed their eyes, and Travis voiced their fervent prayer. "Our Father in heaven, help us follow You faithfully as we begin our life together. Let us serve You with all our hearts. Tomorrow, help Beth be the confident person You've developed, and thank You for the families who have helped to make her mine. Thank You for all Your blessings, Lord, especially for our Christian families and for the hope that comes from You. In the name of Jesus, amen."

Raising her face to look into her eyes, Travis lowered his mouth to hers, and in their last tender moment until they were husband and wife, they gave themselves to each other in their hearts.

Travis pulled away and touched her cheek. "Good night, my golden girl. Tomorrow, you will be mine."

A Letter To Our Readers

Dear Reader:

In order that we might better contribute to your reading enjoyment, we would appreciate your taking a few minutes to respond to the following questions. We welcome your comments and read each form and letter we receive. When completed, please return to the following:

Fiction Editor
Heartsong Presents
PO Box 719
Uhrichsville, Ohio 44683

1. Did you enjoy reading *Hearts Twice Met* by Freda Chrisman?
   ❏ Very much! I would like to see more books by this author!
   ❏ Moderately. I would have enjoyed it more if

   _____

   _____

   _____

2. Are you a member of **Heartsong Presents**?   ❏ Yes   ❏ No
   If no, where did you purchase this book? _____

   _____

3. How would you rate, on a scale from 1 (poor) to 5 (superior), the cover design? _____

4. On a scale from 1 (poor) to 10 (superior), please rate the following elements.

   ____ Heroine   ____ Plot
   ____ Hero   ____ Inspirational theme
   ____ Setting   ____ Secondary characters

5. These characters were special because? _____
_____
_____

6. How has this book inspired your life? _____
_____
_____

7. What settings would you like to see covered in future
   Heartsong Presents books? _____
_____
_____

8. What are some inspirational themes you would like to see
   treated in future books? _____
_____
_____

9. Would you be interested in reading other **Heartsong
   Presents** titles? ❏ Yes ❏ No

10. Please check your age range:
    ❏ Under 18   ❏ 18-24
    ❏ 25-34   ❏ 35-45
    ❏ 46-55   ❏ Over 55

Name _____
Occupation _____
Address _____
City, State, Zip_____

Schoolhouse Brides

4 stories in 1

The lives of four schoolmarms are complicated by unexpected encounters. Can these women find a place in their hearts for love? Titles by authors Wanda E. Brunstetter, JoAnn A. Grote, Yvonne Lehman, and Colleen L. Reece.

Contemporary, paperback, 352 pages, 5³/₁₆" x 8"

Hearts♥ng

HEARTSONG PRESENTS TITLES AVAILABLE NOW:

___HP352	*After the Flowers Fade*, A. Rognlie	___HP460	*Sweet Spring*, M. H. Flinkman
___HP356	*Texas Lady*, D. W. Smith	___HP463	*Crane's Bride*, L. Ford
___HP363	*Rebellious Heart*, R. Druten	___HP464	*The Train Stops Here*, G. Sattler
___HP371	*Storm*, D. L. Christner	___HP467	*Hidden Treasures*, J. Odell
___HP372	*'Til We Meet Again*, P. Griffin	___HP468	*Tarah's Lessons*, T. V. Bateman
___HP380	*Neither Bond Nor Free*, N. C. Pykare	___HP471	*One Man's Honor*, L. A. Coleman
___HP384	*Texas Angel*, D. W. Smith	___HP472	*The Sheriff and the Outlaw*, K. Comeaux
___HP387	*Grant Me Mercy*, J. Stengl		
___HP388	*Lessons in Love*, N. Lavo	___HP475	*Bittersweet Bride*, D. Hunter
___HP392	*Healing Sarah's Heart*, T. Shuttlesworth	___HP476	*Hold on My Heart*, J. A. Grote
		___HP479	*Cross My Heart*, C. Cox
___HP395	*To Love a Stranger*, C. Coble	___HP480	*Sonoran Star*, N. J. Farrier
___HP400	*Susannah's Secret*, K. Comeaux	___HP483	*Forever Is Not Long Enough*, B. Youree
___HP403	*The Best Laid Plans*, C. M. Parker		
___HP407	*Sleigh Bells*, J. M. Miller	___HP484	*The Heart Knows*, E. Bonner
___HP408	*Destinations*, T. H. Murray	___HP488	*Sonoran Sweetheart*, N. J. Farrier
___HP411	*Spirit of the Eagle*, G. Fields	___HP491	*An Unexpected Surprise*, R. Dow
___HP412	*To See His Way*, K. Paul	___HP492	*The Other Brother*, L. N. Dooley
___HP415	*Sonoran Sunrise*, N. J. Farrier	___HP495	*With Healing in His Wings*, S. Krueger
___HP416	*Both Sides of the Easel*, B. Youree		
___HP419	*Captive Heart*, D. Mindrup	___HP496	*Meet Me with a Promise*, J. A. Grote
___HP420	*In the Secret Place*, P. Griffin	___HP499	*Her Name Was Rebekah*, B. K. Graham
___HP423	*Remnant of Forgiveness*, S. Laity		
___HP424	*Darling Cassidy*, T. V. Bateman	___HP500	*Great Southland Gold*, M. Hawkins
___HP427	*Remnant of Grace*, S. K. Downs	___HP503	*Sonoran Secret*, N. J. Farrier
___HP428	*An Unmasked Heart*, A. Boeshaar	___HP504	*Mail-Order Husband*, D. Mills
___HP431	*Myles from Anywhere*, J. Stengl	___HP507	*Trunk of Surprises*, D. Hunt
___HP432	*Tears in a Bottle*, G. Fields	___HP508	*Dark Side of the Sun*, R. Druten
___HP435	*Circle of Vengeance*, M. J. Conner	___HP511	*To Walk in Sunshine*, S. Laity
___HP436	*Marty's Ride*, M. Davis	___HP512	*Precious Burdens*, C. M. Hake
___HP439	*One With the Wind*, K. Stevens	___HP515	*Love Almost Lost*, I. B. Brand
___HP440	*The Stranger's Kiss*, Y. Lehman	___HP516	*Lucy's Quilt*, J. Livingston
___HP443	*Lizzy's Hope*, L. A. Coleman	___HP519	*Red River Bride*, C. Coble
___HP444	*The Prodigal's Welcome*, K. Billerbeck	___HP520	*The Flame Within*, P. Griffin
___HP447	*Viking Pride*, D. Mindrup	___HP523	*Raining Fire*, L. A. Coleman
___HP448	*Chastity's Angel*, L. Ford	___HP524	*Laney's Kiss*, T. V. Bateman
___HP451	*Southern Treasures*, L. A. Coleman	___HP531	*Lizzie*, L. Ford
___HP452	*Season of Hope*, C. Cox	___HP532	*A Promise Made*, J. L. Barton
___HP455	*My Beloved Waits*, P. Darty	___HP535	*Viking Honor*, D. Mindrup
___HP456	*The Cattle Baron's Bride*, C. Coble	___HP536	*Emily's Place*, T. V. Bateman
___HP459	*Remnant of Light*, T. James	___HP539	*Two Hearts Wait*, F. Chrisman

(If ordering from this page, please remember to include it with the order form.)

Presents

Great Inspirational Romance at a Great Price!

Heartsong Presents books are inspirational romances in contemporary and historical settings, designed to give you an enjoyable, spirit-lifting reading experience. You can choose wonderfully written titles from some of today's best authors like Peggy Darty, Sally Laity, DiAnn Mills, Colleen L. Reece, Debra White Smith, and many others.

When ordering quantities less than twelve, above titles are $2.97 each.
Not all titles may be available at time of order.

HEARTSONG
PRESENTS

If you love Christian romance...

You'll love Heartsong Presents' inspiring and faith-filled romances by today's very best Christian authors...DiAnn Mills, Wanda E. Brunstetter, and Yvonne Lehman, to mention a few!

$10.⁹⁹

When you join Heartsong Presents, you'll enjoy 4 brand-new mass market, 176-page books—two contemporary and two historical—that will build you up in your faith when you discover God's role in every relationship you read about!

Mass Market 176 Pages

Imagine...four new romances every four weeks—with men and women like you who long to meet the one God has chosen as the love of their lives...all for the low price of $10.99 postpaid.

To join, simply visit www.heartsong presents.com or complete the coupon below and mail it to the address provided.

✂ -

YES! Sign me up for Heart♥ng!

NEW MEMBERSHIPS WILL BE SHIPPED IMMEDIATELY!
Send no money now. We'll bill you only $10.99 postpaid with your first shipment of four books. Or for faster action, call 1-740-922-7280.

NAME _____

ADDRESS _____

CITY _____ STATE _____ ZIP _____

MAIL TO: HEARTSONG PRESENTS, P.O. Box 721, Uhrichsville, Ohio 44683
or sign up at **WWW.HEARTSONGPRESENTS.COM**